Avery Press

New York • London

Deep Wicked Freaky

Deep Wicked Freaky First Print Edition, 2014.

Cover design: Brandon Stout.
Author photograph: Troy Aossey.

Avery Press, USA.
Manufactured in the United States of America.
Copyright © 2014 Landon J. Napoleon
All rights reserved

ISBN: 0988651971
ISBN: 978-0-9886519-7-5

Deep Wicked Freaky

LANDON J. NAPOLEON

"Weird, funky, and offbeat… *Deep Wicked Freaky* is a harrowing, hysterical, and ultimately life-affirming romp through America's dark and desperate underbelly. Landon J. Napoleon's prose is gritty, jagged and full of passion."

—David S. Goyer

Praise for Landon J. Napoleon's debut novel *ZigZag*:

"One of the boldest and most original first novels to appear in a long time. It's also very funny, in a way that only the raw street-song of truth can be funny."

—Carl Hiaasen

"A remarkable debut… An unaffected, moving, astonishing insight into the heart of a troubled, silent genius."

—*Kirks Reviews* (starred review)

"… this mixture of comic adventure and paean to the values of volunteerism is a vivid read. An impressive debut novel…"

—*Library Journal* (starred review)

"Landon J. Napoleon conveys the strength of the human spirit through his wonderful creation, and in the process tells an engaging and enriching story."

—*Barnes and Noble Discover Great New Writers*

"… a latter-day *The Adventures of Huckleberry Finn*. Like Twain's classic, this novel excels at adolescent monologue."

—*Arena Magazine*

"… an affecting tale of the triumph of hope over desperate circumstances… a modern day *Of Mice And Men*."

—*The London Times*

Praise for *The Rules of Action*:

"Briskly told and well-drawn... this legal thriller does what many courtroom-based novels and television shows do not: It stays true to the actual practice of trial law... A fast-paced tale of justice in action and a remarkably accurate portrait of a trial lawyer's daily grind... Prospective law students are frequently encouraged to read law-student memoirs or legal hornbooks, but for a realistic view of litigation and a great deal more action, they'd do well to add this legal thriller to their reading list."

—*Kirks Reviews*

"One of the most compelling and entertaining books I have ever read on the strategy and gamesmanship of the legal process."

—Former Arizona Attorney General Grant Woods

Praise for *Burning Shield: The Jason Schechterle Story*:

"This true story reads like a novel."

—*Kirks Reviews*

"...[an] inspiring true story of triumph."

—*Publishers Weekly*

"Landon J. Napoleon displays a flair for detail in this fast-moving book... an inspiring read."

—*The Arizona Republic*

"A powerful, inspiring story of one man's will to survive and to thrive in the face of horrific injuries. It is also a keen look into the workings of our police men and women and the close bonds that knit them together. We admire them, and we especially admire Jason Schechterle."

—Janet Napolitano, former Arizona governor (2002-2009) and Arizona attorney general (1998-2002)

"Sad, exciting, life-changing and emotional... an amazing story of one man's triumph over tragedy with the support of an entire community."

—Jack Ballentine, former homicide detective
and author of "Murder for Hire"

Books by Landon J. Napoleon

Novels

ZigZag
Deep Wicked Freaky
The Rules of Action
The Flatirons

Nonfiction

Burning Shield: The Jason Schechterle Story
Angels 3: The Karen Perry Story

www.landonjnapoleon.com

For my Dad, the original dreamer

Preface

IN THE EARLY 1990S, at the outset of my writing career, I was teaching a course at a local college. One of my students was a convicted felon who'd served his time and was trying to get his life back on track. He told me in detail about what he'd been sent up for: driving stolen cars from Phoenix to Las Vegas. From there, I learned how the setup worked, from start to finish. A seed was planted: What would it be like to drive a stolen car across the desert, alone, in the remote blackness?

Years later, in 1998, I'd sold my first novel, *ZigZag*. I began writing the follow-up in 1999, which was the original template of the book you now hold. Getting from there to here, however, has been quite a ride—not unlike driving a stolen Porsche across the desert, alone, in the remote blackness.

Concurrently, I was headed for an emotional crossroads and a subsequent internal voyage that forever altered the course of my life. While I had finally achieved my boyhood dream of being an author, I now had equally difficult and vital work on the spiritual front. In emulating my heroes—the writers, musicians and other creative artists who struggle with inner demons and mapping a life course— I was right in step.

Around that time, I dreamed the phrase "deep wicked freaky," scribbled it down upon awaking, and later discovered it to be both the theme and title of the novel I'd already begun. I finished the first draft in August 1999 and, amid untangling various personal discoveries, finished a second revision in June 2000. Looking back, it's clear the emotional business of the day was clouding my creative abilities. Neither draft was ready for publication.

Meanwhile, like some precocious honor student, my debut *ZigZag* was off doing amazing things. In January 2001, David Goyer (of *Blade, Batman Begins* and *The Dark Knight* fame) began filming his adaptation of *ZigZag*. He invited me to the set and graciously allowed me to stick around for the entire shoot. While watching John Leguizamo, Oliver Platt and Wesley Snipes bring my novel to life every day, I began a third revision of *Deep Wicked Freaky* while on the set of *ZigZag*.

In July 2001, my agent began submitting *Deep Wicked Freaky* to publishers. Two months later 9/11 happened, and publishing was effectively shut down. Subsequently, it seemed that timing, market forces and world events conspired against the book's publication. More than a year later, in December 2002, I began a fourth revision as the book was still evolving. But by the spring of 2003, my own creative juice for the story had ebbed. I put the manuscript aside and wondered if I would ever return to *Deep Wicked Freaky*.

Over the next years, *Deep Wicked Freaky* was wholly off my radar. In late 2004 I met a prominent plaintiff's attorney and began a five-year collaboration that eventually became the legal novel *The Rules of Action*. Then, without explanation, in early 2011 the Literary Gods rang with a simple and somewhat mysterious directive: *Deep Wicked Freaky*. It was time to bring the story home.

Two decades after the initial idea, I plowed back into the manuscript with renewed clarity, energy and fervor I hadn't had since writing the initial draft. Timing, of course: All the years of work on the unseen structure of my psyche had brought me to a new place of peace and creative freedom. Work continued on the novel through the year and into 2012 when my publisher first released *Deep Wicked Freaky* as a digital edition only. Now, for 2014, you are holding the first print edition of the book, a work more than 20 years in the making from those initial seeds. Welcome to my world and career, where life is lived almost entirely in *process*.

Although not a straight sequel, *Deep Wicked Freaky* is a follow-up to *ZigZag* because of the connecting thread between the two books: the strong-willed Jenna Jet from *ZigZag* takes the lead in *Deep Wicked Freaky*. This is her voice, her story, her spirit—a triumphant narrative that's intertwined with my own long journey, wild fancies, dark nights of the soul and a long search for the steadying anchor we each must find. Ultimately, that journey can take much longer than we ever anticipated at the outset just as it took many years to finally bring Jenna Jet home.

I'm hopeful you enjoy the ride.

—Landon J. Napoleon, summer 2014

Part I

Ante Up

Chapter One

DEEP WICKED FREAKY.

Says how you go nine times no snags and end up here on number ten: 4:58 a.m., California wasteland, grooving through black desert in a stolen Porsche 911 Turbo, after-market Polk Audios pumping new Pantera, palms wet on leather, burning a Marlboro, pressed block of crisp C-notes on the back end when Bobby B takes title in a few hours if— and it's the Queen Mother Bitch of all ifs—the headlights in the rearview aren't wired to CHiPs, Jon and Ponch and pals looking to take you down.

Says how getting a cartoon name is why you trade three weeks and ten times for a cool hundred grand, how you get goose eggs from Rolle until you close it out and drop coupé in LA.

Says how one-in-three Papa Jet goes 77 years, and you find out he's alive same week he's scheduled to die, same week you decide to start boosting imports. Welcome to the 1990s.

The music keeps pushing, all alone on a highway where beat-down yucca will kick your ass for a drink of water. Gap the window and blow smoke. Stub glowstick in the ashtray. High beams bearing down, familiar sick feeling gnawing below the belly button again, eyes strain for any detail about who's back there. You put the window up.

Joker right on your tail.

Money-sniffing dogs looking to take you down.

You got the game to keep it together and stay cool?

Just stay cool.

The thundering pulse of the music, soundtrack of your life.

Two thoughts. One: You are not a car thief, at least not an official one. Two: You are not a car thief, official or otherwise, unless you get caught.

Double-Blind, Two-Box Lock-Up.

Porsche Tiptronic S: downshift to Fourth with a flick of your thumb, no clutch, hands never leaving the wheel.

Take a hint, loser.

Headlights full-frame.

Go around, just please go around.

Cut music.

Airtight silence except vague road hum, the precise whine of German engineering cutting black air.

Pedal tap, flash taillights. A thousand promises about how you'll never do anything like this again to a God you never talk to when you're holding a rubber-banded cash roll.

Normal people are in their beds right now.

You're not a normal person.

BOOM, red and blue bursts against black morning sky, the whole world collapsing in and sucking you down toward some unseen darkness, thumb-shift to Second, right side of the sparkling new Porsche spitting rocks just off the pavement, speed-yellow slab of Stuttgart's finest cocked sideways as you roll to a stop.

Engine idle.

You think about firepower.

Pantera flash: "Here we come reach for your gun!"

You think about a 9mm Browning automatic pistol with a fifteen-round clip. Oily heft. Hammer cocked. Pad of your index finger resting on the trigger just like Rolle showed you.

You hate thinking about guns.

You think about it because that's the only gun you've ever held in your life, the only gun you've ever shot. You think about how they make it look easy in the movies and how in real life you aim at a Coke can and squeeze off a clip from 25 feet without hitting anything.

You think about firepower you don't have because the best thing to do is usually the opposite of whatever Rolle says, every time telling you, just in case.

Just in case what?

Just in case this.

You had the speedometer locked in two over the limit, like always, so no way it's for speeding. Maybe just a routine stop.

Cross the California state line.

Nice man asks if you have any oranges today.

You try to remember the last time the citrus police nosed in with night-vision goggles and red laser sights.

Maybe Border Patrol looking for illegals.

Yeah, illegals always sneak into the USA one at a time in $115,000 imports because there's so much trunk space to hide family and friends.

Rearview, silent red and blue flashes.

You can't stop staring at what makes you sick, the lights, and the next thought twists your stomach in new ways, ways you've never felt.

Cop door slamming back there.

Footsteps and a flashlight beam.

You're a twenty-something woman on a deserted strip of desert asphalt: maybe cops aren't your worst fear.

Chapter Two

HERE'S WHAT ROLLE SAYS after you both do bong hits: Three weeks, ten cars at fifteen a pop, 60/40 split. A normal person laughs and tells Rolle he's stoned. And crazy. And stupid.

You're not a normal person.

Normal people don't cross over and dip down into the ugly side of life.

Barter it.

Sell it.

Give it away.

Jordan telling you, uglier the mash, sweeter the cash. Hit them with the ugly tax babe because you see and do a lot of ugly. Why did you listen? Thinking back always makes you cry. You're on the other side now, but you can never fully scrub out the stain. Something they took away you can't get back.

Wear nothing but a G-string and carry around a feather duster. *Seven hundred.*

Loose-change Charlie. Forty-five-minute drive on icy roads, and you're lining up little stacks of quarters, dimes and nickels. Baggies full of change, because it all adds up the same way. *Five hundred.*

After, how many nights you'd drive away, tears. Telling yourself, you're not a bad person. This is not who you are. OK, then who are you? Same answer keeps coming back.

You're not a normal person.

You're watching *The Brady Bunch* (Greg hides a goat in the attic) on the 52-inch Rolle got for making a dude's invoice disappear at Meryl Mack's. You wonder how three boys and three girls share one bathroom, and what happened to your *Brady Bunch* family with a dad who's always there to untangle problems inside a sitcom slot?

I ain't lying, Rolle goes. Know this dude who knows this dude Bobby B from England who's out in LA and pays cash for hot cars. But the thing is, only if they on Bobby B's list, and the only way onto the list is you get referred by someone on the list. Bingo on referral: Rolle knows a dude on the list. Your end would be sixty grand. Then he goes, you couldn't make 60 grand in three weeks if you were squatting golden eggs. Charming visual.

Killing time for four months with a dude who spends his days at Meryl Mack's, where they paint any car or truck for $199. Rolle is the only black guy you've met who would rather chill to Johnny Cash than Public Enemy.

Rolle doesn't know anything about your old life because you lied. Thinks you were a secretary at a record company back East. You told him you saw Johnny Cash in the hallway one day at the office, all by himself buying a Three Musketeers from a vending machine. Rolle was, like, in complete awe. You're not a huge liar about everything, but Jordan also told you there's a difference between secrecy and privacy. That was maybe the one thing Jordan ever said that still makes sense.

The pot makes you foggy. Yeah, duh, but 60/40 what?

Straight up, he goes. He's got the hook-up. You run all the cars. Plus—now he's smiling that smile you just have to love—Rolle holds all the money until the end, you know, like an escrow company.

What the hell's a what?

You know, third party keeps the money iced down until the end so everyone stays true to the dream.

You really have no idea what he's talking about.

The dream, according to Reginald Clifton Rolle (you've never heard him called anything but "Rolle"), is to parlay the windfall into opening his own detailing shop. Paint and pinstripe cars. A place to express his artistic nature. For practice he painted cartoon characters on the side of his van. Daffy Duck smoking weed, mostly, and trying to nail that cute little girl duck with the eyelashes and fluffy behind. He can draw really good. Now asking, so what do you think, you down with this Bobby B thing?

You smoke pot to forget about things you don't want to think about, but somehow that's what always floats back. Like that there's a one-in-three chance you have any biological connection to Papa Jet.

One in three.

Worse odds than you got at the Atlantic City tables. Not exactly what you want when you step up to select your gene pool. Papa Jet's boy (your supposed Dad) and Mom, both American, move to Holland or something because Dad has a government job with the U.S. embassy or maybe the State Department. If you ever see him you might have a better handle on his actual job title.

Mom picks the day you get your first period for the big news flash. You're 12 years old, standing in that scummy bathroom that's always freezing cold with the toilet that drives you crazy because it never shuts off and sounds like someone torturing a cat. You're trying to figure out the instructions that came in the box. There's no lock, so you lean with your back against the door to keep mom out. She's been knocking for the last ten minutes and asking a hundred times in her drunk voice, you sure you're OK?

You try a few times, but something doesn't feel right. You're only 12. Why do you have to figure everything out on your own? Fine. Whatever. Ease up on the door a little.

Mom tumbles in.

Her booze breath makes you turn your head. The cigarette in her hand has an inch-long ash about to drop. She takes the tampon and shows you how, the cigarette dangling next to your leg still with that ash. Then she's all hugging you before you even have a chance to pull your underwear up. Something about crossing the threshold into womanhood like this is somehow a good thing and you just won a contest or something. Whatever.

You just want her to get out of the bathroom and pretty much your life, but this is when she tells you about Amsterdam, how she was seeing two other men besides Dad when she got pregnant with you. You're all, thanks, Mom, for the great news.

Congratulations, it's a girl.
Congratulations, it's a girl.
Congratulations, it's a girl.

AS you hold in the smoke you talk in that funny voice and tell Rolle you're confused. Blow out the hit. You drive ten stolen cars across the desert, and he wants a bigger cut for *knowing* a guy on a list? The driver, if anyone, should get the good end of 60/40. Driver does the real work, driver puts in the time, driver takes all the risk. You're not sure how you know this, but it sounds logical. Part of your brain is also still thinking about that golden egg thing and wouldn't that be totally cool if you could actually do that? With pot it seems totally possible. And then a glimpse of reality.

You're not a car thief, official or otherwise.

You tell him there's no way you'd ever drive a stolen car to California. And ten? Forget it. Not worth the risk.

If nothing else, Rolle is way easy on a girl's eyes. He wears his hair real short, everything pushed forward tight on his head. He's wearing Revos (he's always in sunglasses—pushed down onto the tip of his nose—except when sleeping), jean shorts and a tight green fluorescent T-back shirt. He's all bulging muscles and rock-hard midsection and bright white teeth. Picture a body hard as kitchen cabinets with a model-pretty face. One look and you're hooked. Only after the sex is so good do you discover Rolle's three passions in life: cars, weed and the music of Johnny Cash.

Four months.

You never thought he was going to be your actual new life, but you didn't think you'd chill here this long either. But one thing: Rolle is the first person you have normal sex with after everything that happened back East.

Normal sex is when you don't have to ask for money up front. Normal sex is not wondering how many gross diseases you probably just caught. Normal sex does not end with you wanting to get away as fast as possible and take a shower so hot it practically burns your skin off. Normal sex doesn't end with you crying yourself to sleep every time.

When you're 19, before escort, you try to do 12 different guys in one year. For free. For fun. Why the hell not? A contest with Jordan. It turns into the Mr. Calendar Contest. One guy for each month of the year.

Mr. January.

Mr. February.

Mr. March.

For the year, though, you only make it to October, not all 12. After, you're like, what a dumb contest. The worst part is that you can't take things like that back. Whatever you did or didn't do is already out there. Most times now you don't cry after sex, but sometimes. Rolle is always nice and tries to comfort you while he pokes at the bowl on the bong. But eventually he drifts away without saying anything and goes to watch TV. After you fall asleep you dream about digging in the dresser drawer for Rolle's gun. Full clip, rack the slide. Take aim like he showed you.

You know it's a dream because you hate thinking about guns.

You aim at everything you can't stand from your old life and squeeze the trigger. There's no noise or flash, no bullets, no blood. But the cool thing is that everything dark from before just dissolves and then turns to television static. Those few seconds right as you wake up and open your eyes give you a quick glimpse of what a normal person feels like. A little flash of peace before you realize. It never lasts more than a few seconds, and then the Real World is back.

You're not a normal person.

Rolle nods. OK, yeah.

OK, yeah, what?

OK, yeah, I'd give you the big end of 60/40.

This is your life.

You're not sure, but you're starting to think he's actually serious. You don't say anything because what scares you more is you're starting to think you're maybe actually considering this, too. All you can think about is what all that money could buy: freedom. A whole new life. You reach for a little perspective.

BONG HIT.

This is just for fun, right, so you do the numbers in your head: 60 percent of $150,000 is $90,000. OK, let's round it to $100,000 to me and $50,000 to you. This is fun!

How you figure on that one?

Even thirds: I get two for driving and you get one.

Damn, girl, you pretty quick on the mathematical uptake.

Deal?

Deal.

So how would it work?

OK, he goes, gig goes down like this. You'd be the runner, first link in the chain that moves late-model imports from Phoenix to LA, a six-hour blast give or take. Phoenix, Rolle goes, is number one in the country for stolen cars. You know one gets boosted like every 18 minutes here?

No, you don't know about these things.

Yeah, since we been smoking like two cars been stole.

Your brain just goes, that's weird: should we call the police? And how will those people get home? Then a pause, and your fogged brain is back on the golden egg thing again. That would be so rad and so much easier than working. Just pop one out when you're low on cash.

OK, he goes, doesn't matter you don't know cams from crankshafts. Leave that to yours truly. All you need to know is that every time you drop a freaky-hot ride in LA, you fly back to Phoenix fifteen total, ten to the good. That's tall cash, baby, shrink-wrapped in plastic.

You're all, tall cash?

Fifteen thousand dollars.

Fifteen thousand?

In six hours.

Six hours?

Six hours.

That is a golden egg.

That's what I'm saying.

Chapter Three

THE FLASHLIGHT BEAM IS SO INTENSE *you use your hand like a visor. You can't tell if he's a real cop or some impersonator who pulls women over and then like three weeks later, outskirts of some one-gas station town, farmer's dog nosing your naked body (minus head) in a soggy cornfield. No head means the cops don't close the case for seventeen years, when they raid a nasty basement apartment on an unrelated warrant and cha-ching: There's your freezer-burned face behind a pint of ice crystals used to be Cherry Garcia. Supermarket tabloid headline:*

Missing head found!

"Where you in such a hurry to get to this morning?"

C'mon, two over the limit? "Can I see your badge?"

"How about can you answer my question first."

"After I see your badge." You give him a weak smile. He does nothing; just stares. "I know my rights."

"Your rights..."he says, laughing. "That's a good one. You're on my highway, my rules. Your rights? Look here."

He points the flashlight up at his badge. He's fat and has a dark moustache speckled gray. But other than that, who knows what a real badge looks like anyway?

"Now where you headed?"

You're still trying to figure it out: a cop with an attitude, or headhunter impersonating a cop with an attitude? This is definitely how various body parts end up in basement freezers. You just say, "LA."

"Where you coming from?"

"I do something wrong?"

"Just answer the question."

Pantera flash: "Here we come reach for your gun!"

But what comes out: "Phoenix."

You're staring straight ahead as two trucks rumble by, one each direction. You smell dust and watch the speckles shimmer across the Porsche's halogen beams. The sun will be up soon. Your throat is so tight you can barely speak, fear wrapped all around you now, screaming in a dream where no sound comes out. You look at him. He leans his head left and right, then back at you: "This your car?"

No. No, no, no, no.

Stay cool.

Think fast.

Breathe.

Talk slow.

Confidence. Say everything with confidence. "Nah, it's my boyfriend's."

Slowly now, wipe wet palms on jeans.

"Must have a few bucks, this boyfriend." He's nodding his head. "So what's he all about?"

"What?"

"The boyfriend."

"What does he have to do with anything?"

He chuckles. "Sooner you figure out it's me who asks the questions out here, the better. For both of us."

You let out a long sigh and scratch the corner of your mouth for effect. Your heart is thumping hard and fast. Just like you and Rolle practiced all those times with him as pretend cop. "He's in sales."

"Kind of sales?"

"Medical. Supplies. You gonna give me a ticket for being two over the limit?"

"There you go again, young lady. Questions, questions, questions. You studying to be a lawyer or something? Freaking lawyers. That why you like to ask so many questions? We got us a little lawyer lady here?"

"No."

"OK. Now, I say anything about a ticket yet?"

"No."

"No I didn't because we're just getting warmed up here."

You think about firepower.

You hate thinking about guns.

Squeeze your index finger until the clip is empty, rack locked open and smoking, cordite dust. Yeah right, Jet, you can't even shoot a can. You're not shooting a cop or a headhunter or anyone else.

What you're doing is going to women's prison for a long time.

Grand theft auto.

Felony charge times ten.

Damn pot. Ideas that sound brilliant when you're stoned are usually the exact opposite in real life.

Chapter Four

AS SOON AS THEY FIND OUT about the unborn you, possible Dutch dads #2 and #3 are all… however they say goodbye over there. A month after you're born, somehow "real" Dad finds out about Mom's affair (she never tells him about Dutch Boy #3). She doesn't even know how Dad finds out about #2. Dad is not a happy expatriate. Ships Mom and the baby you stateside, files for divorce and cuts you both off.

Mom picks up the bottle and a job cleaning office buildings in the city. Mom says Dad refuses to take a blood test to see if you're his, and she doesn't force things. Dad doesn't say anything because you never see him. Mom says maybe you have dual citizenship until you're 21: Dutch and American. Mom says she's not sure what you are now. Mom says apply for a passport and maybe they can tell you. Normal people don't have to apply for a passport to figure out their nationality.

Now Rolle is all into it. Stealing cars, he goes, ain't as easy as it used to be a few years back in the 80s. Slim Jim your way in and pop out the ignition. Or cut a duplicate key and go. Now cars getting better security systems than the White

17

House. Security's moving a whole new direction. Talked to a dude the other day said there's this new thing in Massachusetts called LoJack. Rad name, huh: LoJack. It's like a computer tracking device leads the cops right to your car. And you can't take it out, somehow they build it right into the car. A minute ago, like '88, they got federal clearance to start putting that bad motha on cars outside Massachusetts, and now they in Florida, he thinks. The window to boost cars old school about to close. That's coming for real, girl, but it ain't gone nationwide yet.

They're also starting up with these smart keys with transponders built into the head of the key and a rolling code that changes the signal each time to the starter and ignition. You believe that? The other bitch is the key itself, which ain't like no regular key. These keys are, like, three-dimensional with laser-cut grooves milled out all the way around. Bet you in ten years every car will have them. Split-tooth in an apron at the hardware store won't even be able to make you a duplicate key anymore. Dude at the dealership will even be like, what do I look like here, Mr. Wizard? They'll have to send the keys out to a specialist. It's all coming, guarantee you on that one.

So truly, we in this transition period. Technology's out there, it's coming, some cars got it, but most still don't. Now just to be safe you just pick up the damn thing you want to steal—literally pick it up and flat-bed it—and drive that way to the drop point. Except flat-bedded imports draw big-time heat. One at a time, though, if you can break through the security system? Now that's the way to run cars below five-0 radar: You're just another Jimmy rolling big wood.

Big wood?

From driving the Porsche, baby. That's what it do to any man.

What are you, like an expert at stealing cars now? When did this happen?

I know people and people know other people who know things. We around cars all day and when you around cars you talk cars. Painting, tuning, fixing, stealing. All the same game. Just listen, baby. OK, two ways to unload hot cars: chop shops and foreign resale. Chop shops go after the vehicles everybody driving, but got no style. Honda Accords and Toyota Camrys. Minivans and SUVs, which are just overpriced minivans for people who are all, I ain't driving no minivan, so where's my SUV? Baby, you ever see me rolling up in a minivan, just pack your things and go. What else we got?

Lexus.

Hundred coats of paint, baby, don't make a rice burner anything but a rice burner. I got nothing against my Asian brothers, but someone please tell me who can be styling in that? Here's a hint: You want a Toyota, then save the money and buy a damn Corolla.

You go, how about Jaguar?

Two words: Grey Poupon. Old rich white dudes smoking curvy pipes look like they for weed.

That's more than two words.

Give me another one.

Audi.

I want a VW, baby, I'll get us that bus they got with that full kitchen setup, little fridge and a pop-top.

Saab.

Too easy: basically that is one ugly-ass automobile.

Lincoln.

White trailer trash and brothers who can't afford imported style.

Cadillac.

American junk, same as Lincoln.

Ferrari.

Sure, that V-12 will put the tingle in your ding-ding, but where you put the groceries, baby? And what kind of pimp wants to pay $300 for an oil change?

OK, Mustang.

OK, you got me a little there. That Shelby Cobra 427, can't say anything about that one. But see, here's the thing: that Henry Ford? Dude hated Jews. So only natural he hated the brothers, too. Why you think he built all those black Model T's? I'll tell you why: servitude. Black serving white. It's sneaky, but that's why. No self-respecting black man can drive a Ford anything, it's like driving a damn Klan car. Same with BMW. You know they were all cozy with the Nazis, too? You think Nazis be down with the brothers? No way I'm driving a Nazi car either.

Lamborghini.

What am I, ordering Italian? That come with a white-wine cream sauce?

You're crazy.

So anyway, he goes, chop shops strip cars down to the frame and sell off the parts, wheels, body panels, you name it, like to garages that ain't exactly on the up-and-up. Know what I'm saying? They get the parts deep discount and re-sell them as new on repair jobs. You go in to get a little fender-bender sorted out and never even know you driving away with stolen parts. It's like Frankenstein's laboratory except with cars.

Frankenstein?

But forget about all that nickel-and-dime, baby, that ain't what Bobby B's all about. Bobby B's into hustling slick rides out the USA and moving them overseas. This is where you come in: You drive across the desert to LA, Bobby B drops dime, loads 'em on a boat, and sells them to the bad brothers in Japan and Australia and Thailand. Export some Euro style to my Asian brothers with a deep discount. Everybody's happy. Global economy, girlfriend.

Freedom. Enough money to start your new life once and for all, a life where you don't ever have to do ugly things for money. *BONG HIT.* The THC in your brain works up this one, and you share it with Rolle: Total freedom is not having a reason *not* to run ten stolen cars.

That's exactly what I'm saying! See the beauty is, Rolle goes, even though everyone gets a little bump along the way, no one's really getting hurt. No violence. And no one's talking about giving crack to a kid, right? No, we're talking about boosting a tight Bimmer worth a buck and a quarter from some dude who's got 312 cholesterol and too much damn money and, besides, insurance company buys him a new one. He's probably ready to upgrade anyway. Perfect set-up, baby.

What about the insurance company, don't they get left holding the bag?

Rolle pauses and then smiles. Name one person going to lose sleep over some insurance company opening the checkbook?

Good point.

You ever hear of an insurance company going bankrupt?

No.

That's because it's the biggest racket out there. They practically printing they own money. About time the people took back a little of what's rightly ours. We gotta revolution, baby.

You laugh. He always makes you laugh especially when you're stoned. But wait. Why doesn't Rolle just run the cars himself or get one of his car buddies?

See that's the thing, baby. This way we keep it in the family and both take a cut. Set us both up for a long time. And besides, hot mama like you the ace in the hole.

How?

Proven fact. You're what gets us past "Go" every time.

How's that?

Women, especially fine women like you, got a lot better chance getting off if the cops pull you over. Mark my words on that one, baby. When you packing fine 34Cs, you free and clear all the way to the ocean.

Chapter Five

"NOW LET'S GO ONE STEP AT A TIME: License, registration and proof of insurance."

Documentation.

Now he wants actual documentation.

Stay cool, breathe, except no matter how hard you try to play it cool, your face gives you away. He knows you're guilty, you know he knows, he knows you know he knows, so why not just end this torture now and turn yourself in? You can't take any more. You open your purse and hand him the license, your hand visibly shaking.

"My license is valid."

Oh my God, what a dumb thing to say. He checks the license and gives you a look. You know he knows it's a phony that you saw this guy make in his apartment. An Arizona license with your face, different name, and the same address as the real owner of this car. Then the cop leans down, his free hand where the window disappears into the door, the other hand moving the big flashlight around the interior: nothing but a black purse on the passenger seat. Standard car-boosting procedure: toss everything.

Everything.

Rolle goes, that means the owner's manual to the box of Kleenex jammed under the driver's seat to the $19 designer stainless-steel travel mug. For reasons you can't pinpoint, your gut's telling you he's a real cop, which makes you glad you didn't bring the gun. Then again, that means HE'S A REAL COP! Or is he?

Headhunter.

"OK, now how about that registration and proof of insurance?"

"Yeah, no problem." Glove box. You hesitate. You can't do this. Yes you can. No you can't. Shut up, you're doing it. No you're not. Get out in front of this before it gets worse. You can't show him paperwork because there isn't any paperwork. Everything's bogus. The only truth is that your whole life is one big lie and this is just more lies. From birth you've been a lie, thanks to Mom and Dad. Now you've stacked up a string of lies that stretch from Europe to the East Coast to here and back, and guess what? Now it's all over. Rolle once said, you ever get pulled over just give the officer an eyeful of your gorgeous rack and that smile. He goes, that set of headlights could get Charles Manson paroled. Only Rolle could get your boobs and Charles Manson in the same sentence.

So what you have, in addition to your driver's license, is a proof-of-insurance card and registration they make up on the computer with your fake name and the right VIN and the right address. Cop can run your plates: clean because the owner's drooling into his 600-thread count pillowcase when the gig goes down. That's the window where you live each time: the six to eight between lights-out and coffee talk. A car's not stolen, officially, until someone reports it stolen. You're wearing a tight T-shirt, no bra, everything directly in the flashlight beam. You've never felt so pathetic. So alone. So stupid.

"Look... officer, I know you're just doing your job, but my boyfriend... you know, I'm just headed out to LA to see some friends, do a little shopping. We had a blowup, he doesn't know I took the car, but... is there any way you can cut me a break here?"

He runs the flashlight down a little and then back up, then looks at your license again. A car passes as he leans into the open window. "Let's see, hair: brown. Eyes: green. Five-four, huh? 1-0-5." Except he stretches out the zero into a long ohhhhhhhhhhh.

Maybe you weighed 105 in the eighth grade, but not any time since. Last time you stepped on a scale, three weeks ago, the dial screamed past 120 and stayed past. You leapt off before it could settle. First time you cracked that barrier. You haven't gone near the scale again.

"You brunette all over?"

OK, real cop or headhunter, he just officially crossed the major creep line.

You feel your entire body go cold.

Your throat goes dry.

He waits a few seconds before handing you back the license, and you pretend to ignore his last question (answer: yes). He pulls away, keys jingling on his belt, then everything quiet except the idle.

Heart pounding.

You slide the phony license back in the little zipper pocket inside your purse. The flashlight beam is gone, except your head won't move to the left, frozen, as though not looking will make him disappear and put everything back the way it was before Harrison West. Before Manifest Destiny. Before Rolle.

You're not a normal person.

What's the cop doing? What's happening here? Random flashes: Thumb-shift through five gears and see whose car is faster? Go for the little can of pepper spray in your purse? Punch the creep in the nuts?

"I got me some suspicions ever since I saw you in this serious ride, all alone, this time of morning. Be a cop long enough and you just sort of know how to smell when something don't add up. Even when everything on paper lines up. Know what I'm saying?"

"Not really."

"Not really. OK, you start asking questions like how a little thing like you and this here car get put together."

"I said it's my boyfriend's."

"Exactly. That's what you said. Don't mean nothing. Like maybe what really happened is you and the salesman boyfriend are doing things you shouldn't being doing. What did you say he sold?"

"Medical supplies."

"Right. That your little code for maybe you're running dope up from Mexico? Maybe I tear off one of these yellow quarter panels and find 100 kilos of premium green?"

"No, officer, I swear—"

He cuts you off by holding up his hand and shaking his head.

"I suppose you're praying right now that I'll let you off with a warning? Let you drive off, no strings attached? That what's rattling around in that pretty little noggin of yours?"

You're not sure if you're supposed to answer or not. Hearing him say "pretty" makes you cringe. You may vomit here any minute.

"Not go digging around the glove box, look the other way if maybe you boosted this car from the boyfriend? Or maybe you and the boyfriend are in on it together? Running dope. Stealing cars? Who knows God what else you might be into?"

You shake your head, no.

"I don't know, young lady, lot of unanswered questions here. And you're asking me to look the other way?"

"I'd really be grateful, officer."

"You should be, I do all that." *He's standing in close, running the beam around the interior.* "Yessiree, that's a tall order to fill. Tall order indeed. You're sitting between that proverbial rock and a hard place as far as the law's concerned."

You stare straight ahead and don't say anything because he's right, which means you're looking at a lose-lose proposition: You're busted unless he's willing to deal, and if he's willing to deal, you know he's not going to ask you to sign up for community service. You have to really concentrate to keep yourself from throwing up all over the tightly stitched and buttery-smooth black leather.

"Well, maybe today's your lucky day. Suppose we did work something out? No more questions. Let you get on your way."

"That would be so great. I'd really appreciate it." *Except you're afraid to ask what he means.*

Deflect and delay.

Try to come up with an escape plan.

Try to keep from hyperventilating.

Breathe.

There's a pause that extends into a drawn-out moment. Maybe it's over, he's about to cut you a break. Are you dreaming? Are you really here?

Sharp clunk on the door.

Metal flashlight.

"So how about if you step out of the car, young lady. You just ain't convinced me you ain't up to no good."

Chapter Six

ROLLE IS, WELL, ON A ROLL.

See, mostly the cars come from valet parking lots at the snob resorts in Scottsdale, the Beverly Hills of Phoenix. Think about it: Where else do the owners of the baddest luxury imports drive up and walk away from their six-figure rides with the keys dangling in the ignition? Crazy mothers are practically asking you to steal the car.

So, while Mr. Trust Fund and Ms. Fake-Boobs-and-Hairspray are elbow-deep in dirty martinis and chateaubriand for two, we got a valet dude passes the key to another dude in a van. Check this out: generic white van outside, full-on precision milling shop and electronic lab inside. Dude says the inside looks like NASA stamped out that bad boy. And to run the key? We ain't talking no dropout works part-time at the Home Depot; we're talking electronic lab tech who can laser-cut a perfect duplicate of any Porsche or BMW or Mercedes key out there. Bobby B doesn't say where he gets the key dudes or how much he pays them, but word is he buys them away direct from import manufacturers. Picture a dude in a white lab coat with black-rimmed glasses who can make us a key, do your trigonometry homework *and* program your VCR all at the same time. Bobby B just gets the same brothers that already know how to laser-cut a precision key, read the ID code on the microchip and stamp out a perfect duplicate, complete with electronic transponder in the head of the key, inside of 30 minutes. Slip that duplicate in the ignition, and the car thinks you're Hammer Time, Too-Legit-To-Quit, because all the electronic codes between the chip coil and induction coil are dialed in tight. Right dude at the right money will blow that up every time.

Rolle pauses like you're supposed to clap or something. Boy stuff. You smile and nod.

Anyway, while Hans the locksmith engineers a new key, valet dude copies down the car owner's name and home address from the registration, which he gets right out the glove box. Thirty minutes later, duplicate key goes in valet dude's pocket, original back on the hook. Two hours later Mr. and Ms. Look-At-Us-In-Our-Guess-Jeans tip the dude just made their car.

Next few days, two-man pick-up team cases the car. Late-night drive-bys to see when the car's accessible, does it get garaged, what time? See, lot of time rich people leave their cars out because they got too much shit: bratty teenagers got they own BMWs, jet skis, bunch of them little sailboats, boxes of old crap they don't need, trailers, his-and-her Harleys, treadmills that are just $2,200 laundry racks—

You get the idea on the full garage.

Anyway, best time to make a pick-up: 2 a.m. The workaholics finally passed out and the self-talking-visualizing overachievers won't be up for at least three hours. Pick-up driver gets dropped a block away, moves in on foot, opens the car door with the duplicate key and drives away. Rolle holds up his hand even though you weren't going to say anything: don't even sweat the engine noise, baby. You think some fat stockbroker clone bowed out from cold calls and single malt gives a shit he hears a car 2 a.m.? Or some anorexic babe who's stiff from yoga and groggy from guzzling merlot with her cookie-cutter friends? Neighbors? Yeah, right. Rich dogs don't even give a damn they so fat and lazy from too much people food.

People food?

Yeah, you give a dog waffles for breakfast and smoked salmon for dinner he gets fat and lazy. Anyway, so while rich dude's cruising slumberville our driver's already rolling up to the West Side. Now each vehicle got what they call a VIN, 17-character vehicle identification number.

You think about trying to stop him, but it seems like too much work.

Tenth character in a VIN is the model year starting with *A* for 1980, but here's the thing: they leave out certain letters because you might confuse them for numbers, which is why there's no *I*, *O*, *Q*, *U* or *Z*, which is why if your ride's an '88, your tenth character is a *K*, not an *I*.

More boy stuff; does he really think you care?

You're thinking about Mom's call. Yesterday. No way, you think, when you hear her booze voice on the answering machine, but you pick up when she says she has something important to tell you. Mom never has anything important to tell you. In fact, Mom never has anything to tell you, hasn't called since you left. She says she just got a call from Dad, that the nursing home called and said Papa Jet has taken a turn for the worse, but unfortunately Dad is in meetings all week in Beirut.

You're all, what? Who the hell is Papa Jet?

Dad wants to know is there any way Mom can fly out to Phoenix to start the final arrangements. Mom says how your grandfather's 77, how she doesn't really know him except she heard stories that he was supposedly a country singer and would you mind? She's already giving the address, which is just up the road from here.

You're all, country singer? Papa Jet is my grandfather?

Next thing you think is, what a bastard you have for a father. His own dad; why isn't *he* on the next plane out?

Then Mom, what a capital "B." First time she's called in four months? To dump this on you?

You get the information and hang up.

Now you're thinking, whatever. No way, not now.

You're three weeks away from $100,000 and your new life.

Total freedom.

Time to close the door on an old life you didn't do anything to deserve.

Normal people visit their sick grandpa. Normal people don't get 1-in-3 odds that Grandpa *is* Grandpa. Normal people would know 1-in-3 Grandpa is in a nursing home less than five miles from where you've been staying the last four months. You know the answer before you finish the thought: *You're not a normal person.*

Chapter Seven

"STANDARD POLICE PROCEDURE," *he says."Come on. Let's go."*

Do you get out, or make a run now? No, Rolle said never run. Never, never, never. No matter what because car always loses in car versus helicopter. But do you get out? "Then you'll let me go?"

"Sure. Let's go."

He opens the door and stands there. You're having trouble breathing, but through the haze you see your options clean and simple. Go along or go to jail. Get this car to LA or get nothing. Maybe it's finally time. Stop running from your past. The lie that started when no one would claim you as their own. Draw the line. Stop digging the hole any deeper and just let him haul you in.

Surrender.

Your world's fuzzy and not quite real, like a dream, as you watch yourself climb out of the Speed Yellow Porsche, close the door, and get your first good look.

Fortysomething.

Burly.

About 20 pounds to the bad.

You're still not even sure he's a real cop. Car looks real enough, silent red and blue flashes. Not that real or not real matters much now: He's holding the lever. Long black flashlight back in your eyes.

"Over there," he says, waving you around to the passenger side of the Porsche, still idling. "Up against the car."

Hearing that makes you want to cry, but you rub your eyes to stop the tears.

Then you give him a short stare and shake your head before turning and laying hands on glossy Speed Yellow rooftop. First time he frisks you it seems pretty legit like he could really be doing his job. OK fine. This is worth a walk. See, no drugs, no guns, nothing. Adios.

Second time, though, he's over the line, and you both know it: flashlight tucked under his left arm, hands everywhere they shouldn't be, up and down your legs, front and back, then up top again and around in front.

Sick. Throat parched back to silence. You couldn't scream now if you tried.

"Spread 'em," he says, kicking your legs apart. Steel-toed boot catches the inside bone on your ankle, sharp twinge up your leg. Tears. Lots of tears now.

You hold your head up toward the sky so he doesn't see. OK, is this worth a walk? You don't get an answer, just more tears. Get a badge number, turn him in. Yeah, right after you drop off this stolen Porsche.

Light is starting to crack the horizon except not enough that anyone in that SUV headed this way can see what's going on over here.

Leather creaking, keys jingling.

Crappy cologne.

You fight back the lump rising in your throat. You turn your head slightly and dry-heave into the black desert. Flashing red and blue. Small white cross near the pavement edge. Flowers tied to the cross with string. Burned-out and dangling upside down. You look away, at a bright light in the sky. Star? Planet?

Meat hooks finally leave your body.

Boots scraping gravel on pavement.

Acid bubbling up in your throat.

Eyes blurry.

You can't look, wondering if a little roadside grope will put the ape back in his cage, or if that was just a warm-up for his chimp stick.

Headhunter?

The only sound is the idling engine.

The only smell is the exhaust drifting this way from the low, rumbling tailpipe.

The only thing you feel: numb and nauseated.

You turn and look at him, rounded Porsche taillights glowing red on his face. You hold your hand up to shield your eyes from the flashlight beam and step back toward the road. The sick feeling in your stomach is coming back with more bad news. Your voice barely working, "We done?"

"Just about." He takes your arm, cold metal around one wrist, then the other, ratcheting cuffs, points you back toward his cruiser. "Let's step into my office."

Chapter Eight

A NORMAL PERSON WOULD HAVE a lot of questions when they're about to start one of the more risky lines of part-time work.

You're not a normal person.

You only have a few questions. You're doing bong hits when you get answers.

Why not just rent a truck and drive a whole load of cars out to California in broad daylight? Truck drivers have to stop at weigh stations, sign papers and answer questions. Signing papers and answering questions? Not when you're boosting cars, baby.

Why take the risk of driving across the desert; why not just steal cars that are already in LA? He already do, lots of them, and now he's expanding his reach into other markets. Besides, what does he care if a runner gets bagged and tagged en route? We're all just foot soldiers in the trenches, disposable plastic pawns to the five-star grandmaster.

Why run the cars at night when there's less traffic, maybe more suspicion? That's the best time to get a big head start, slip out of state and be halfway home before Cole grinds Colombian beans.

Is it fifteen grand no matter what car? Like, if a $50,000 BMW is worth fifteen to Bobby B, shouldn't a $115,000 turbo Porsche be worth 30? Already axed that one, too, like why not a commission structure based on Kelley Blue Book instead of a flat rate, right? But all that came back was that if I want a percentage then what about helping on the fixed expenses like vehicle storage and transport and, oh, by the way, all the dirty palms Bobby B has to grease to get the cars out of the country.

That was three weeks ago. If the questions ever seemed important, it was three weeks ago. Now your life is locked in a narrow groove at 200 miles an hour. Twenty-five foot concrete walls on either side. You can't go left, you can't go right. Luke Skywalker trying to off the Death Star.

Stop, you get destroyed.

Slow down, you get destroyed.

Only way out is straight ahead. Push the accelerator through the floor and let the road vibration carry you to the other side.

The freedom of $100,000.

Each time starts here in the middle of the night, greased-out industrial area off 35th Avenue. Single-story warehouses and broken-down buildings tacked together with corrugated sheet metal. The rusted neglect of economic oppression. Chain-link fences topped with ratty barbs. A sticky, roofing-tar smell hanging over everything. The unending sound of barking dogs pissed off from junkyard living and, Rolle says, unlike the rich dogs, *not enough* people food. You drive along a cratered dirt road that takes you deeper into the industrial maze. This is where the Toxic Avenger might winter. Rolle parks *America's Ride*, engine idling.

deep wicked freaky.

Says how you end up here: 2:15 a.m., hot September blackness, West Side pick-up point, one last car for $100,000, Jet eyeballs times two scanning hard. No moon, just black ink. Radio man just said it's 104 degrees. AC sputtering: sweat trickle down the center of your back.

"Something's wrong," you say aloud, biting your lip and staring into the night. Car's always here when you get here, unlocked, keys on the driver's-side floor. Nine times in a row.

"Maybe they got popped on the way," Rolle offers, which does nothing to THC your nerves. Or maybe Rolle got the wrong pick-up address. Pick-up and drop spots constantly shifting around, Bobby B always on the move.

Exasperated sigh. You hate yourself already for doing this again. You do this a lot: say you're not going to do something and then do it anyway. The burden of hate you have for yourself growing like a tumor you have to lug around.

Stomach twinge, eyeballs times four through smudged windshield: headlights cutting hot night. You lean forward and watch, and when you see a second set of headlights turn in behind the first car, your heart starts to jump.

"There we go, baby," Rolle says, giggling.

You feel like you're going to throw up. Hot car at 25 yards.

Your first was a Vesuvio Metallic Porsche 911 Turbo.

Always parked deep enough in the maze that cops can't see it from the main road. Rolle tells you the California drop address, different every time in case you get tailed. You memorize the drop address and directions. No paper, Rolle says, in case you get clocked and popped.

Clocked and popped. Story of your life.

Rolle goes into the glove box and pulls out the 9mm Browning automatic pistol, drools like a rain-coater with his nose fogging peep-show glass: Speed Yellow 911 Turbo, sleek German slab of Stuttgart's finest that will make an insurance company see 115,000 shades of red, baby, all-wheel drive. Twin turbochargers and a water-cooled, horizontally opposed flat six. Rolls out of Zuffenhausen with 420 ponies, but stroke and bore the cylinders you can pimp the giddy-up to 500. Zero to 60 in four-point-two and back to standstill in two-point-six. On a dime with those internally vented, cross-drilled brakes. Factory stock governed to 155, but it'll push 200. He drops the clip to check and pushes it back in. Racks the slide.

Live round in the chamber.

Just in case, baby.

You think about it every time, and every time you shake your head.

You hate thinking about guns.

You'll just hang here until they're gone. You've never met these guys, no thanks. Flick ashes out the gap. There's no way you could do any of this without nicotine and caffeine, but especially nicotine. And caffeine.

Someone getting out of the Porsche, door slamming, and walking back to the waiting car. Then another door slamming and the car backing away with nothing but two orange glows. Then the lights are gone. The industrial maze is dark again, a junkyard dog barking nearby.

Time to strap in, stolen Porsche 911 Turbo. Speed Yellow exterior, Rolle says, with carbon fiber and Graphite Grey interior. The sick feeling in your stomach twists again. Too much pressure. Too much riding on the next six hours. Now looking straight ahead, the gleaming Porsche parked about 20 feet away, an alien craft out of its element. You turn and look at Rolle.

"All right," you say.

"All right. You got this baby."

A million thoughts flash through your head, a thousand things you want to say. All you do is manage a weak smile and climb out of *America's Ride*. Even before you reach the car, paranoid Rolle is already backing away, parking lights only he says, in case the cops have the place under surveillance. That's pretty much how it goes with the men in your life: parking lights only.

Walking toward a stolen car worth more than a lot of houses. Heart pounding, gravel crunch, slick palms as you reach out and slide one hand along the cool, glossy gleam of stolen Stuttgart steel. Weird rush of adrenaline and fear and nausea that makes your head throb like drinking a milkshake way too fast. Door unlocked, key under the driver's mat, buttery leather womb. Weird kind of rush when you slide into the cockpit. Leather wrap. First thing you notice, the ignition is left of the steering wheel, and you stick the key directly into the dashboard, not the steering column. Rolle gave you the whole history how that's left over from Le Mans when drivers started the race outside the car and would jump in, left hand finding keyhole, right hand grabbing stick. Your head buzzes, palms sweat.

You're about to roll the dice.

Would you trade six hours for a shot at $10,000 cash?

How about times ten and $100,000?

All you have to do is drop clean.

A normal person would walk away right now.

Yeah, you already know.

Nine times the run from Phoenix is cake: I-10 west straight across the desert. Pushing that line back as far as you can, running hot through the silent black morning, alone, your life on hold for 360 minutes. Straight through LA until I-10 dead-ends into the ocean and dumps you in Santa Monica.

All the cars you've run have German blood: BMW, Porsche and Mercedes. Look-at-me status products that bring guaranteed cash when you show up at Bobby B's with an elephant caffeine buzz and a B-52 crick in your neck from craning the rearview.

Chronological: 1) Porsche 911 Turbo; 2) Mercedes CL600 two-door coupe, black with a V-12; 3) BMW 850C Si two-door coupe; 4) Porsche 911 Cabriolet; 5) Porsche 911; 6) BMW 750iL four-door sedan; 7) Porsche 911 Cabriolet (identical to number four except this one was Zenith Metallic Blue and number four was Guards Red); 8) BMW 850C Si same as number three (stolen from some pro athlete); 9) Porsche 911 Turbo; 10) IN PROGRESS: Porsche 911 Turbo.

All or nothing: fly back to Phoenix with a shrink-wrapped pack, plastic because Bobby B swears there are German shepherds at the airport trained to smell cash. Or it's over just like a cartoon, title of your life story.

You think about freedom.

Total freedom.

Enough money to start your new life, and this time no more ugly. Three weeks ago, ten cars sounds impossible. Then each time a little easier. Getting numb to it. Never as easy as Rolle said, like zipping down to Circle K for a carton of Marlboros and a cold pack of Mickey's Big Mouth. Be back in 20, baby.

Yeah, right.

Eyeballing what the bowed-out oncologist won't discover until you're on the California side of $115,000. Stub butt, blow smoke.

OK, it's time.

Push the key into the ignition on the left, fire the engine.

Twin turbochargers and a water-cooled, horizontally opposed flat six.

You don't know what it means, but you know it's something good when you hear and feel the precise rumble. Parking lights, stick to AUTO mode. Your stomach is really twisted, mouth full of dry oatmeal.

Four hundred miles to sand and foam.

Idle. Not like a car that can hit 185. You're low to the ground in what feels like an airplane cockpit. You pull away slowly so you don't gravel-ping the undercarriage.

Number ten. 2:31 a.m.

The pick-up team always delivers with a full tank of gas, and you've got enough supplies stowed to take you through the first pee break. That stop will be in about two and a half hours, the rest area at mile marker 53 on this side of the California border.

You avoid gas stations and other consumer transaction points where Highway Patrol are more likely to congregate and maybe run random plates when they go slack-jaw at 3:45 a.m. They especially like to run plates on Speed Yellow 911s driven by babes like you.

Two thoughts. One: You are not a car thief, at least not an official one. Two: You are not a car thief, official or otherwise, unless you get caught.

You're definitely not a normal person.

You're heading south, I-10 west just ahead, checking the rearview and moving to the right lane. Hardly any traffic, but this car gets looks from all directions. This is the worst part, the six-hour mental grind. I-10 west on-ramp, drop down to Second with a quick thumb-shift, squeeze down the accelerator through the turn.

You glide through Fourth and Fifth in a flash and then switch the stick to AUTO mode once you're on the freeway. You're less likely to get into trouble without the temptation to downshift and blow past slower vehicles. In this rig, every single vehicle tracking black is a slower vehicle.

You flip on the stereo and hit PLAY, the CD already loaded up. New Metallica. Soundtrack of your life.

Cruise control locked in.

Porsche humming.

For now, all clear in the rearview.

You reach between your legs and lift the 64-ounce Diet Coke you got at Circle K on the way over to the pick-up. Caffeine: key ingredient on all-night desert runs. And then more caffeine. And Marlboros.

You wipe your palms on your jeans.

All clear in the rearview, no headlights. You love no headlights. Rhythmic road thump of the evenly spaced expansion joints.

Thump-thump.

Thump-thump.

Thump-thump.

OK, easy. Breathe. So far, so good. But what does that mean, really? Nothing. Nothing means anything until you drop six hours from now.

Six hours?

Yeah, six hours.

Holy shit.

I know.

You're still soaked in city shimmer, but all you think about is the black night ahead and the sticky web the empty highway holds.

Chapter Nine

DRIVING STOLEN CARS ACROSS THE DESERT is a mind game that takes you beyond terror. Each run twists your head a little more.

Number ten, no question, worst of all. So close, which means you've pushed your luck beyond the snapping point. You do that a lot in life, push things in ways you shouldn't. You're an all-or-nothing kind of girl. Go all in and summon the river card you need. Your mind now locked in a little mental prison, an eerie place you keep crawling back inside. Why do you do this? You hate it, you love it. The warm familiar bed of your own suffering, Dale called it. Dale. Dale makes you smile.

Back east, seven months ago, totally hot Native American, 6-foot-4, beautiful skin, gorgeous black hair tied back in a clean ponytail halfway down his back. He cooked at a cheesy restaurant back home called the Grub and Grog. You know this because you were getting paid to do unspeakables with his sleazeball boss. The Toad.

In three months, Dale never tries to make a move. You do little stuff, hug and hold hands, but it's more like a friendship thing, not boyfriend-girlfriend. Meanwhile, while Dale's grilling filet mignon, you're looking to get the hell out of Dodge. You meet him for coffee at this funky little place you never knew existed. Dale knows more about coffee than anyone you've ever met. In fact, Dale knows more about everything than anyone you've ever met.

You and Dale meet after work and go clubbing together. Dale always pays your cover and buys your drinks. You offer to pay, but he just flashes that smile and shakes his head. Dale doesn't do X or coke. Every dancer you know is always pushing you to do a little bump, help keep you going in those ridiculous heels. You suspect trying it once would be a bad idea and lead you into an abyss worse than the hole you've already carved out. No thanks.

You and Dale go out at 4 or 5 a.m., breakfast at the *Waffle Shack*, which is where you met Dale for the first time. Dale is the bomb because he's the one who really starts you thinking seriously about your new life. First one who helps you sort of believe you can do something better with your life. If you were a psychologist you'd say he's probably like a missing father figure, a man who goes beyond wanting to see your tits and ass.

A normal life where you are a normal person.

Dale talks about awareness and mindfulness, things that at first you said no way because usually the next thing is people are all in your face with Jesus this and Jesus that. Dale never once directly mentions Jesus, but you get the feeling Jesus would totally groove on Dale.

Three months later, you get awareness.

You just sort of wake up one day and right when your eyes are opening you hear this little voice, not your own, but it's there and just goes, it's time to get out of here and do something different. You're like, OK, whatever the hell that was.

But at coffee Dale is your human decoder ring, tells you to just pay attention because maybe that's the first time you've ever heard your spirit.

You're all, spirit?

Spirit, guides, angels, God, universe, cosmic intelligence, The Force, whatever you want to call it. Hmmm. Maybe if you don't meet Dale, you miss the nudge completely. Maybe you don't stop your old ways and take a step toward the new. Dale helped get you out.

Four months later, you get yourself back in this car thing because you think it will get you out for good. Expensive cars driven across the desert for $15,000 shrink-wrapped. That's when it comes back, what Dale said, crawl into the warm familiar bed of your own suffering. Definitely. Then it's back to what you've always heard: You're just a dumb, fat cow who deserves what she gets. You are so stupid. Who are you kidding with this "new life" *crap? You wish you could crawl out of your own skin somehow and just be somebody else better, no more torment of being you.*

Awareness.

Speed Yellow.

Number ten.

The stress pulses around you like a clawing apparition, some hell-bent sense that in about five seconds you're going down. Five seconds pass. Nothing. Then it comes back.

Clocked, popped and locked down.

Three-to-five. Or who knows how long for grand theft auto.

You buzz on these runs in a way you've never felt. Sixty seconds is your entire life, a little snapshot you can see and hold start-to-finish, bam, there it is. Then maybe your life ends, bam, gone.

Wake up and feel the thing and do it. You're alive, girl! Adrenaline pump beyond sex or weed or anything else you've ever felt. Maybe that's why you signed up for ten times. Maybe that's a sign you've run out of good ideas about how to feel like a normal person.

Out here, six straight hours, each 60-second block a divine offering. Surrender. Hold it, protect it. Get down on your knees and pray. One down, hundreds more to go. Two down, hundreds more to go. Three down, and on and on. But you don't focus on the hundreds, you focus on the one. The one is all you have.

Oh my god, shut up. Just shut up already.

Breathe.

Every set of headlights, coming and going, Grim Reaper in blue? Fear swelling to a crescendo as the headlights approach, saucered, passing, harmless, a momentary reprieve until, seconds later, rearview: two more beams cutting night, closing in, closing. Over and over and over again.

Nothing but baked asphalt and slithering hardscrabble between Phoenix and LA. Alone. Origin of Species in a bottle. Four-lane highway, two lanes cut each way with a sun-hollowed strip of earth between, straight through miles of tabled hell. Twisted strips of retread rubber scattered like an anthropologic map of fallen beasts, bleakness beating everything back to the edge. Just you and flannel-shirted Peterbilt drivers and ribbed-out coyotes all trying to make it one more mile marker.

One more minute.

One more hour.

One more day.

Steal something from the devil's clutch, something you can hold, six straight hours of tip-toeing around squeaky floorboards.

Enough. You shake your head and crack the window for some air. It's too hot outside to leave it open, but you take a couple of deep blasts. Window back up, AC notched full, try to force your mind to go somewhere else.

Yeah, you wish.

Blast of Diet Coke and crack the window for a smoke. Rolle tells you not to smoke in the cars because Bobby B doesn't want polka-dot Marlboro greetings via leather.

Too bad. Bobby B can come do this himself sans smokes if it's that important. You light up and think about the run into Santa Monica, straight shot. Same as always. Drop point: I-10 west until you run into the Pacific, just before the freeway ends, exit onto Lincoln Boulevard and make a left; ten blocks down on the right is a Dairy Queen and behind the DQ is a garage; Bobby B will be waiting in that garage with $15,000 shrink-wrapped. It all sounds so easy when you look at it like that.

Drop clean, and you're free.

Santa Monica.

The last time of all last times for everything. If that makes sense. It does to you.

You've been there before. Wouldn't be a bad place to start your new life. Right on the ocean with a wide, long beach to call your own. Winding cement walkway where you'll Rollerblade in shorts and a bikini top. That is, after you lose at least fifteen pounds. Malibu just to the north, Venice to the south.

You flick ashes and take a deep drag. Santa Monica College is right off Pico, and UCLA's not too far away. Many nights alone the last four months studying the map of your new life, Santa Monica right at the top of your list.

Close proximity to Beverly Hills and Hollywood.

Doesn't actually mean anything in your day-to-day reality, but hey, it's your new life. The biggest draw, no question, live in a city that borders the Pacific Ocean, the westernmost border of your own Manifest Destiny, the farthest you can get away from your old life and still be in the lower 48. That feels good.

Number ten. 4:10 a.m.

Speed Yellow Porsche 911 wound and locked at 79, Jet wrapped in Graphite Grey leather, halogens glowing white letters on green:

Blythe 101, Los Angeles 321

OK, give or take, 321 miles of 18-wheeled grooves between you and the end of all madness. The big green signs like old friends you can trust, whispering, you're still rolling. Still free. You're not stopped on the dark side of the road. You pass a sign: Burnt Wells Rest Area Closed; Next Services 35 miles. Volume down on Metallica, mixing now with the sound of the road as you roll west.

So far so good.

You think about those 60-second blocks, each one ticking by and stacking up behind you, no headlights in the rearview right now, nothing up ahead. Just you cutting a Speed Yellow path through the nothingness. OK, yeah, you're going to make it. Not cocky you're-going-to-make-it. Just, yeah, you'll be all right. Then, no, no way you make it all the way to the ocean. Never happen.

OK, breathe.

Relax.

Nothing in the rearview.

You're cool. Just chill, Jet.

You steer with a knee and pull out another cigarette and light. Warm desert air through the window gap. Then you think, maybe you'll make it, maybe you won't, but way too early to start thinking about that. The highway is all still out there unrolling for you to cross.

Tick.

Tick.

Wondering, can you really pull this off? Blow smoke and trance out at the rhythmic snap of white lines. Thinking, that's a damn good question.

Chapter Ten

FIRST TIME YOU MET BOBBY B he says he's named after the famous Scottish poet Robert Burns except forget that, he heard the same crap jokes all through school near Glasgow. So when he moved to America he changed it to Bobby B, no period. No Robert. No Burns.

You tell Bobby B he's got nothing to worry about here because Americans don't read books much less poetry; they watch TV. This makes Bobby B laugh. He's impressed that at least you know Robert Burns wrote *Auld Lang Syne*, the song everyone tries to sing at midnight, New Year's Eve, half-crocked, no idea what the hell they're singing.

Information comes out of Bobby B's mouth in a thick accent at light speed. You only catch about 70 percent of what he's saying. Like when you find the first drop, dull metal building with tall brown doors that swing out, white sheet of paper with a red circle taped to the building, Bobby B's signal that you're in the right place, deal's on. Although it's never happened, green circle means all bets off, pleased with his little red-green switch and calling it countermeasures.

Heat's coming down.

CHAPTER TEN

You and your stolen ride are on your own.

A small airplane wobbles toward the airport, landing gear down. Brown metal door on the right swings open, and you see Bobby B step out in an all-black get-up, nose bright as a strawberry, leather holster under his shoulder with a gun, walking this way with his arms open, palms up, grin, now waving you in with his right hand. You pull the car in, kill the engine and climb out. He closes the tall door behind you. The room goes black. You did it. You just made $10,000 in six hours. Ledger it.

Six hours of mental anguish and drama ends here, smelly garage covered with white seagull spray, no one else around, just Bobby B moving this way and running a hand along the wide wheel-well flare at the back end of the Porsche like a farmer sizing a steer.

First words out of Bobby B's mouth: "Cakey bampots been bringing me nothing but bingers aw week. But she's no like that, smashing, tiding package this one."

You're pretty sure it's a compliment, but you're not entirely sure. Then he says, "Gie the horn a wee pamp."

First time you hear this, the way it comes out in two beats, *giethehorna weepamp*, you have no idea what he's saying. Translation: honk the horn. After nine times, you know this is one of his little rituals: Bobby B says the sound of a car's horn tells him whether it's a gem or a lemon. You're out of the car. You close the door, lean in and pump it twice.

"Pure dead brilliant, this one. Just brilliant. Who's the wee lass?"

"The wee lass is Jenna Jet, and she's hot and tired." You feel his eyes giving you a good grind-over.

"Ach, tidy package, you are."

You don't know why you say this: "My back's all sweaty. From driving."

"Nae bother."

"You're English, right?"

Bobby B takes a step toward you, his finger up in your face, "I'm no English; I'm Scottish. I'm tired of teachin' ye Yanks yer geography, but if ye should ever accidentally stumble onto a map, you'll see Scotland and England are separated by this wee squiggly line called a 'border.' North of the border is the proud Scots, south are the legions of English wankers."

You're a softy for all things British, the whole king and queen thing, the idea of a more civil and refined time and place. So you ask, "What about Wales?"

"No one gies a right fook aboot Wales."

"It's part of England, though."

"No, England proper is the only thing that's part of England. That's it, nothin' else tae it. England is England."

"So who are the British?"

"Unfortunately, much as it sickens me, luv, we're all technically the British, victims of an evil empire built on a bone-crunching system of wicked imperialism. Much like what you've become here in America."

You're really not sure you follow, and you let it go. You just want to get the money and get out of here.

"We're all British: Scotland, England, Wales and Northern Ireland."

"You mean Ireland?"

"Ach, no, *Northern* Ireland."

"Where they're always shooting each other, right?"

"Aye, not unlike American grade schools and restaurants."

"They're British, too?"

"Who?"

"The Irish?"

"No, the fucking Irish are fucking Irish, from the Republic of Ireland, but those who live in Northern Ireland are British because the daft bampots have no got enough good sense to move to Dublin."

You're completely confused. "I'll take your word for it."

"Right, well, whatever, ye tanned the car clean, this one, so nae bother, luv. It's no big surprise ye're knackered, so let's us nick doon for a wee cup of tea. My treat." Then he sees and translates: good job on the car, you're tired, so let's go have breakfast.

Seems nice enough, but you're nervous. About the whole thing. About just stealing your first car. About getting the money. About getting back to Phoenix safe. You just want out.

"Thanks, I really need to get back to Phoenix."

"Ach, Phoenix? There's nae need to go back there. That's a miserable hot place fer harry hoofs."

Phoenix. Your new life gets sidetracked there, a place the locals call the *Valley of the Sun*.

Duh.

A better name might be Valley *on* the Sun because that's what it feels like. A criss-cross grid of six-lane boulevards lined with convenience stores and fast-food franchises stretching endlessly in all directions with little to distinguish one part of the city from another. Pick a street anywhere in Phoenix, and it looks like every other street. This adds up to mindless square miles of concrete and asphalt and Circle K stores and stucco walls.

Sort of a baby Los Angeles, another big Western ghost town, millions forced into their vehicles by greedy developers sprawling in all directions for cheap land, the nameless living behind blacked-out windows, pedestrians rare as rainfall and thoughtful urban planning, year-round sunshine making people forget they're living in a smog-choked rat wheel.

Although the sun burns year-round in Phoenix, you arrive on the downhill side of the brutal summer that stretches from May to October. Each day, the Earth's nearest star unleashes a white-hot rain of radiation on the desert. The mercury bubbles to 110°F, 112°F, 115°F, even 117°F one day. Not even geckos with sunglasses *and* asbestos briefs risk extended time in the firestorm of heat.

Dry heat or not, summer in the Arizona desert is a red-hot hell. Parking lots become seas of burning asphalt. Steering wheels burn your flesh. The airport shuts down when the inferno of hot air robs planes of lift. Plants and trees and the earth itself wither into a cracked, monotone brown as the sun lords out all moisture. Turns out a Phoenix summer is just as bad as the winter you left: windows and doors locked tight, blinds drawn, cars garaged or, please God, parked in a sliver of shade somewhere. All-out sprint from air-conditioned vehicle to air-conditioned building. Pity the lost souls without sufficient freon flowing in transport and abode.

Harry hoofs.

You couldn't have said it better yourself.

"Ach, come on, hen. One cup 'a tea, and that's you away."

You learn around number four or number five that him calling you a hen is what they do over there. An endearing term, he assures you. Whatever, but you don't see how calling a woman a farm animal can ever be anything but veiled subservience. But more importantly, untangling Bobby B's accent makes your head pound harder, his words coming out in quick blasts that blur together. Last thing you want to do is trigger another spontaneous geography lesson. Or a discussion on how misogyny is rooted in the intrinsically patriarchal Anglo-European model. No, instead you hold out the keys and raise your shoulders, trying now to slip away without pushing any wrong buttons.

Keys drop into upturned palm.

"How about my money instead, Bobby?"

"Straight for the dosh every time, you Americans, never a pause for a wee bit 'a socializing." His face gets redder the more he talks. "Like I'm just sent to collect yer messages."

"I've got a flight to catch."

"Yer face. Don't be a nippy sweetie. It's chock-a-block on the 405 right now. Have some breakfast wi me, an hour or so, and then I'll drive ye to the airport."

Another ultimatum on the table.

Fifteen thousand reasons to go eat strawberry waffles with the sunburnt little Scot. Perhaps a small trade-off, but you just don't want to set a precedent first time out. You smile. He smiles back. You wonder how often you smile when you're angry. But you let go when you realize you don't have the energy to care right now. But you're not giving in: "Thanks, but no. Maybe next time, huh?"

Bobby B is wiry, with a tight stubble haircut and intense green eyes, permanent sunburn on his face, nose in a constant state of peeling, that black leather shoulder harness like on the cop shows. He finally relents. "I'm holding you to it, then. You'll no get yer dosh next time until you come have breakfast wi me. And that's final as cheap vinyl."

Whatever that means. He thinks he's bad-ass and scary, but that's not how he comes off. Seems pretty harmless. You're glad it's him at the end of the line and not some other hairy Neanderthal thug. You nod, but really all you're thinking is you can't wait to get home and take a shower and go to sleep.

Chapter Eleven

NUMBER TEN. 4:34 A.M.

You're rolling past mile marker 53 and into the rest area for your scheduled first stop and pee break. Don't pop the champagne, but a mini-milestone: two hours down, four to go. No Highway Patrol sightings.

No close calls or spooky run-ins.

No parked cruisers clocking speed.

So far, so good.

You wish you felt good, but you never feel good during. You feel good when you see Bobby B and hear that crazy accent and drop keys into shiny palm. Until then, you just feel flat-out sick, borderline puking. Pull off the insanity just one more time. "Never again" rumbles through your head like a bad New Kids on the Block song you can't shake, a permanent echo in your life that never dies. Never again. What a joke you are.

Deep breath as you roll into the rest area.

Rest areas in general are risky places. Even in daylight they make you wary. At 4:30 in the morning, however, female in an exotic car, rest areas are straight-up creepy. You always roll in slow, cut off the music, kill the AC and drop the window halfway to hear and feel the *energy of the place before you park. Switch the Tiptronic S over to manual and get ready for some fast thumb-shifting.*

Just in case.

You scan parked vehicles, trucks, and stay aware for anything that doesn't feel right. Like the weirdo in his Toyota truck with the door open that one time in nothing but boxer shorts and black combat boots, just a dumb look on his face. Gross. There's a high degree of comfort knowing perverts don't have a chance at catching you in this ride. A few times just the sense of this rest area has made you put the window back up, punch the accelerator, and drive right through and back onto the interstate.

Women's intuition.

You can see three big rigs parked side by side, idling, all with running lights glowing. There's only one passenger vehicle parked ahead: a jacked-up pickup with oversized wheels, lights off. Thanks to Rolle, your internal caution light goes off immediately. Before you ran number one, he gave you his typical Rolle breakdown.

See baby, certain rides set off your first-level radar. Here's how it goes in reverse order of cruciality:

1) convertibles

2) pickups pulling trailers

3) 4x4's

4) anything that's been lowered, raised or repainted at home. No way you trust brothers who have that much time to fuck around with their no-class rigs.

No need to sweat SUVs or late-model imports that put the owner back at least $30,000. So how's this shake out?

Old business guy in a Lexus cooling his heels? No problem.

Young guy hanging around his brand-new Ford Mustang? Hmm, keep your eye on him. Same young guy in a brand-new Corvette? Judgment call: makes the money cutoff, but why'd he go so flash, like look at me: no dick, all car.

Black Camaro with racing slicks and a jacked-up tail? That crazy wannabe's cranked up on trucker candy. Guarantee.

Absolute wack: anyone—man, woman or infant child—behind the wheel of a modified pickup.

You remember thinking, infant child?

You pull in as far away from the truck as possible, put the window up and kill the engine. You balance the big Diet Coke cup on the floor and slip out of the car. Gotta pee bad.

Two guys up ahead by the bathrooms, standing in the eerie black silence smoking cigarettes. Maybe truckers comparing hemorrhoid horrors. Or the boys from the pickup. Could be trouble either way. You walk by with purpose and without eye contact. One of them says something, but you can't tell if he says it to you or his buddy. Your heart is racing as you glide by, your palms going sweaty.

Restroom. Five grimy stalls, all so gross you stand there wondering if there's any way you can hold it. But you know the answer: In about 40 minutes there's a rest area at mile marker five, last one before you cross into California. You've stopped there before, on numbers one and two, but for some reason it always makes you too nervous breaking that close to the border.

Cross the California state line.

Nice man asks if you have any oranges today.

Like you're being overconfident. Out here, arrogance will get you canned in one of those 60-second blocks. Just like that.

Custody.

Processed.

Game over.

With that in mind, you take the least-offensive stall, which is a real tossup. You hold your breath, drop jeans and hover-squat over the disgusting bowl with your feet up on the seat.

Champion technique, no contact with anything gross.

You're breathing through your mouth and think about running cars across the desert, hyper-aware, animal sense, like a deer drinking water.

Damn, you can put back a lot of Diet Coke in two hours.

You put down a thick stream for a solid 45 seconds, then wipe and zip up. Out of the stall, you take one look at the sinks and rub your hands on denim. Then back into the darkness where you stop at the soda machine and buy two more cans of Diet Coke just in case.

Now past the smokers without slowing, and then the long walk back down the sidewalk to the awaiting Porsche. You don't ever look back, but you're praying the entire time that they're not following. When you get to the car you allow yourself to turn. Two cigarette glows still back up by the bathrooms, breathing a little easier, heart pumping hard.

You wonder again if you'll survive the next four hours. Break free. Hands shaking from the elephant caffeine buzz. Palms wet when you see another set of headlights turning in and coming this way. Just like that, the ever-present lump in your throat hardens into near-vomit.

Grim reaper in blue?

You'll completely exposed, out of the car, no chance for a getaway from here.

The lights grow brighter, car moving slow now. Seventy-five yards out.

Joker right on your tail.

Money-sniffing dogs looking to take you down.

You got the game to keep it together and stay cool?

White car, shit, could be, your heart really pumping now. Throat parched, brain buzzing.

Car closing: You go deer-in-headlights.

A thousand empty promises about how you'll never do this again and blah blah blah. Never again. Please.

Normal people are in their beds right now.

White car idling, 50 yards, not parked or moving, headlights still beaming this way.

Adrenaline pumping into your brain, mind spinning, reality blurring around the edges except you don't move.

Frozen.

Please.

Nightmare rolls on, acid bubbling up and burning your throat.

White car still straight ahead. Fifty yards and holding.

Only sound is the white car's idling engine.

Only smell is the dusty stillness of a moonless Arizona night.

Telling yourself aloud in a low voice, we're OK, we're OK, everything's cool.

Yet you know you're lying. How can you not be? It is definitely not cool that this car is sitting there idling with its headlights locked on you like enemy radar.

The Porsche is parked with the ass-end facing the headlights, perfect position to run your plate. Perfect position to radio in helicopters and a SWAT team to tag-and-bag Jet times one into oblivion.

You get the sense that it's all over, this is it, and why did you bring yourself into this mess? You want to apologize to yourself before it's too late. Because maybe you're about to get shot to death or something. At the very least you're going to prison. Standoff in the desert.

Please. You stare at the headlights beaming this way. Locked in place.

Heartbeat.

Palms.

Burning lump.

Then a voice coming from behind you, "We give you a hand or something?"

You spin back around to your left: the two truckers, clown smiles, standing five feet from the wicked speed slope on the front end of the Turbo Porsche.

Chapter Twelve

BREAKFAST TO BOBBY B means a balls-out run on the PCH down to Newport Beach, a good hour in the opposite direction of the airport, in a Porsche just like the one you dropped. You are not in the mood for breakfast with Bobby B, but after five times he insisted. Halfway home, what can it hurt? You're elsewhere, thinking about the two-box lockup system you came up with to keep your new life safe.

The Porsche rails through the narrow turns at crazy speeds, the sun still low, cutting in and out of light and shade, cool ocean air rushing through the sunroof. Off to your right, the Pacific shimmers as far as you can see, seagulls floating down toward the water. It's one of those days that makes you regret even more the four months you've been sidetracked in Phoenix.

Go west, young woman.

Bobby B downshifts and takes a turn too fast. The rear-end of the car fishtails and then lurches when rubber grips pavement again. Your knuckles go white from squeezing the handhold. Bobby laughs and pushes the car even harder into the next turn.

"Nae bother, luv. Pure dead brilliant, these cars."

Breakfast.

Small place perched on a cliff, eight tables on the balcony, all empty except yours because of the breeze and shade. You suggested inside, but Bobby B insisted on a table right at the edge of the balcony with the spectacular ocean view. The breeze is strong enough that you press your arms on both sides of the menu to keep it from ending up in the Pacific.

"Three hundred million Americans, and not one of you knows how to make a proper cup of tea. A tea bag dropped in a cup of lukewarm water is just not on. You put men on the moon for fuck's sake; would it kill you to learn how to make some decent Earl Grey in a teapot?"

"See, talking about tea makes you sound very English." You feel Bobby's stare. "Sorry. British, whatever."

"Scottish."

"Fine. Scottish." You warm your hands on the steaming coffee mug. Bobby B is still complaining that the tea water isn't hot enough. You ask, "So how long you been here?"

"In LA? About six months, give or take."

"I meant in the U.S."

"About six months, give or take."

"Straight from Scotland to LA? Quite a change."

"Ach, LA's no that different from Glasgow. Just take away the palm trees, the sunshine, Hollywood, the smog and crime, fake boobs everywhere you look, and all the impossibly good-looking, yet hopelessly superficial people. Then they're pretty much the same."

Bobby B: Hard edges. Needs to buy some sunblock for his face and let the head stubble grow out a bit. Even his scalp is burned bright red. Not really your style, but he's cute in a punker sort of way.

"So," you say. "Question."

"Erect, it's a full two-inches-plus above average, based on the statistical norm of 5.4 inches. I'm pushing eight."

You smile. "About the cars. I mean, how'd you get into this?"

"I'd prefer to continue the conversation about my massive willy in all its glorious girth."

You stare out at the ocean and suck in a deep breath of cool air.

"C'mon, Jet. Take a joke. I'm just takin' the piss. You know the situation. Less ye know, the better."

Three weeks.

Ten cars at $15,000 each.

The less you know, the better. Sounds like the line you'd get whenever you asked about Dad.

"Look, Jet, I can't talk about it. Let's just say crime runs in the family. Ye follow the business wherever it takes ye, and next thing ye know, ye're living in La-La Land and having breakfast wi Jenna Jet. There you have it. It's no very complicated."

"You like it?" You tap out the cigarette and struggle to light another in the gale-force wind.

"La-La Land or the business?"

"Both, I guess."

The waitress arrives with your strawberry waffles with whipped cream; Bobby B gets the meat lover's plate, double meat, no plate. The two pounds of dead flesh kills your appetite.

"So you didn't answer."

"What?"

"About whether or not you like it."

Bobby B pauses, sips his lukewarm tea and looks out at the ocean. "Wouldnay say eechie or ochie."

The wind picks up again, and you zip your leather jacket to your neck. Hot enough in Phoenix right now to kill livestock, and six hours on the road it's cold enough for black leather. Bobby B, in a tight black T-shirt that hugs his wiry little arms, no jacket, doesn't shiver. A seagull lands on the white wooden rail behind Bobby B and walks sideways along the peeling white paint.

"How about you?"

"What?"

"I've been telling ye since ye showed up with that 8-Series, Jet, it's time to move up the ladder. Ye're putting your arse in harm's way every time ye make that run. It's sheer madness, that one. Ye make the move to LA, and I'll set ye up in a much safer position. No pun intended."

You think about what Rolle says after you both do bong hits: three weeks, ten cars at $15,000 each, 60/40 split. Eventually rounding up to a $100,000/$50,000 split. A normal person would laugh and tell Bobby B he's crazy.

"I don't think so."

Progress, not perfection, Dale used to say.

"I'm telling you, Jet, couple years wit me, you'll be set up for life. I got ten people like you running a hundred cars a month just from Vegas and Phoenix. I've got another ten people lined up to work the PCH from San Francisco to LA. At this rate we'll hit my target of 250 cars a month inside of six months. That's $5 million cash a month *after* paying the runners their fifteen grand a pop. My biggest problem now is how to hide and legitimize all this fucking cash. But I'm no complaining."

You take a bite of waffle and push the plate away, light a cigarette.

"I could use a savvy young woman like you out here. I'd create a special position. Pay you top dollar."

"Yeah, special position. Like what, doggy style?"

"Ye're a right cheeky one today."

"Thanks, but I signed up for ten, and them I'm out. For good."

"I'd make you my minister of finance. Know what I'm saying? Ye cannae trust these LA types, not a single one of them."

"This from a man with an ambition to steal $5 million a month."

"I'm no stealing; I'm redistributing wealth."

"Yeah right. Redistributing other people's wealth into your pocket. Except wasn't Robin Hood English?"

Bobby B laughs. "Pure dead brilliant. Ye cannae help but admire the spirit of the 21st century American woman. Bunch of tidy tarts, ye are. What I'm talking about here is straight on the up-and-up. I'd cut you in, Jet. A real piece of the action, straight percentage off our monthly gross." He pulls a pencil out of his pocket and scribbles on a napkin that a gust almost takes away. "You come work for me, I'll give you half a point right off the top. At 250 cars a month, that's $25,000 a month to you."

You're all, what?

You're pretty sure you'll never join ranks with a sunburnt little Scot; you're going to stick with your promise this time and start your new life right. Out for good. Never again. Awareness. But you have to admit that part of you is letting it roll around in your brain a bit too long. All you can do is smile and shake your head at Bobby B.

Two hours later, brilliant daylight, Bobby B's dropping you off at LAX. You're at the curb, cars and taxis everywhere, a woman cop walking slowly this way telling people to move along.

Tired and edgy, Mr. Scottish—British—English—whatever is trying to pawn chump change.

"So when will ye be back out, luv?"

"What the hell's this?"

"Nippy sweetie, don't get yer knickers in a twist. S'all there. Every bloody cent."

A shrink-wrapped block of cash the size of a dictionary sits on your left knee. Fifteen grand in hundreds is small and easy; these small bills are bulky and dangerous.

"Ah, Tam! Ah, Tam! Thou'll get thy fairin, in hell they'll roast thee like a herrin."

You're in no mood.

You simultaneously fight back an urge to punch his face, and eyeball your purse to see if the money will fit. "What happened to the cute little stack of hundreds?"

"Accounting glitch. Too many cars coming in, one of my higher-ups is late with a drop. We're skint. So I had to scramble just tae pull this lot together. Nae need to worry, luv. Fifteen thousand dollars with the full faith and backing of the U.S. Treasury Depart—no, no, don't do that, luv."

You're tearing plastic. "Really don't need this right now."

"Keep the plastic on, luv. From here those dogs can smell a rancid belch in Malibu."

"Tens and twenties?"

"Which are easier to pass than hundreds. It's a one-off, Jet. Next time you'll get the standard."

Next time.

Barter it.

Sell it.

Give it away.

Shot through black morning and then coaxing what you already earned from the sunburnt Scot.

Total freedom.

"So when will I see you again, then?"

He's leaning toward you. You ignore him and try to shove the money block in your black purse. No dice. Bobby B winces when you run your nail file across the plastic.

"Ye're flirtin' with disaster now, luv."

"Yeah, and whose fault is that?"

"Ach, come on, Jet, how about a wee bit of gratitude? Some people work all year tae get what you just made in one day."

"One day, huh?"

Plastic off.

Couple grand in your jacket pockets and the rest bagged and zipped. Too much cash on any flight is a risk, but this bulk is really pushing it. You're out of the car before he can say anything else, your mind focused only on getting back to Phoenix clean.

He's calling your name, but you just keep walking. Before you reach the sliding doors, you hear Bobby B wind up the engine into a high pitch as he pulls away. You turn and watch the car slide past a taxi and speed away, Bobby B's hand waving out the sunroof. He pumps the horn twice.

You're in the terminal now, last leg of the journey that started nine hours ago. Your flight leaves at noon, which gives you just enough time for a couple beers.

The airport cocktail lounge is busy, but you find a seat at the end of the bar. Your purse stays on your lap, straps wrapped around one hand just to make sure.

You order a draft and watch people hustling back and forth. You drink half the beer in one blast, the cool bubbles tickling your throat all the way down. You won't fully relax until you're on the plane, door sealed, wheel chocks cleared, plane belly riding at 45 degrees.

That's when it will be OK to think about your money without jinxing the run. You finish the beer and order another, the bartender giving you a long stare as she takes the empty glass.

What's her deal?

The second beer doesn't taste as good, but almost. You finish, pay the tab (Ms. Happy gets a five-dollar tip anyway) and grip your purse straps with both hands as you leave.

You think about Bobby B's cash-smelling dogs. Cyber-canines with spiked collars crouched behind planters, sniffing out rogue cash. You smile, the beer buzz kicking in nicely as you walk toward your gate.

Part II

All In

Chapter Thirteen

TWO GUYS, BOTH WITH LONG HAIR, one tall and lanky, one with deep acne scars. Acne Boy is staring at you. Tall Boy is the one talking and smoking one of those cheesy cigars with the plastic white tip, which brings back your old life. The Toad. Nothing but bad news there.

"Need some help or something?" Tall Boy says.

"No, thanks, I'm cool." They're standing close enough that you can smell cologne and see the thick razor stubble on Acne Boy. Way too close. They're in your space, and it's making you feel sick.

"No problem, sweetheart," Tall Boy says, walking toward you and giving you another blast of his cherry-cheap cologne that makes your nose tingle. "You on a little trip or something?"

If he only knew. "Not really. Anyway, I'm fine. Thanks."

Tall Boy steps past you and stares at the idling car. "Fuck is this numb-nuts doing?"

Same thing you've been thinking.

White car idling, headlights still beaming this way over your left shoulder. Just slip away before Tall Boy's testosterone stirs the pot. He's still staring at the idling car. "I mean, *what's this prick's problem? Does he want to go? Does he really want to go with me? I'll go if he wants to go."*

"Flip him off, Eddie," Acne Boy says. "Flip him off, see what happens."

Two idiot cavemen pounding their chests might be just what you need. Diversion.

"This your car, sweetheart?" Tall Boy asks without looking away from the idling car. *You turn your head.*

"Look, I don't know you. I just want to get on my way here." *You're not asking permission, you're telling him.*

"Hey," Acne Boy yells, "No reason to get pissy. Just makin' conversation."

You walk around the back end of the car and pause on the driver's side.

"Don't go, sweetheart. Tell us about your kick-ass ride."

Acne Boy gives you a dumb stare as you slide down into the cockpit, door slammed and locked in one steady movement. Your hands are shaking now. Tall Boy is walking around the nose of the car, eyeing you, a panther sniffing prey. You fire the engine and glance rearview.

You check that you're in MANUAL and rev the engine once. Tall Boy's stopped about five feet from your door, still staring, slowing turning the Toad cigar in his mouth.

You back from the curb and pull away, eyes glued to the rearview. The cavemen yell something, but you can't tell what.

Everything cool now.

Thumb-shift to Second.

Except headlights moving in behind you now.

"Shit, who is that?"

You wipe away a tear. If it is a cop, then he's already run your plate, which came back clean. Maybe that's why he hasn't made a move. Then again, something tells you he's not a cop. Either way, you don't want to hang around to find out. Force the hand. Go all in. Push stack to center.

You push the accelerator and the car rockets forward, tachometer sweeping right. You're careful not to flatten the pedal to the floor, Rolle warning you Turbo 911s have more thump than most people can handle. Enough torque that the left front wheel will lift off the ground while the other three still grip asphalt.

Thumb-shift to Third.

Tachometer.

Fourth.

When you hit Fifth, you're at 120 and blinking past the scattered cars and trucks.

130.

140. Hands sweaty, heart pumping, adrenaline dump.

You move way over in the left lane and flash past an 18-wheeler so fast it scares you into releasing your foot completely from the accelerator. Engine winding down.

Rearview, headlights gone. Everything gone.

120.

Thumb-shift to Fourth.

Tachometer winding up.

110.

100. Slow.

80. Like you're stuck in mud.

Ten minutes later you wind the car down and pull off the road until you're off asphalt and hear rocks hitting the undercarriage. You kill the lights, but leave the engine idling. You're parked on a slight slope. You scan the hot, desert blackness, desolation surrounding you, trapping you, laughing at you.

A creepy chill tingling up your back.

A dusty smell in the air.

Everything dried out and dead.

You wait and watch, remembering the rigs and various cars you passed. Slowly, one by one, they trickle by. Accounting. Then you see it, bright flash of red and blue against black morning sky, the whole world collapsing and sucking you toward some horrible conclusion, Stuttgart's finest cocked sideways in desert dirt.

No sirens, just silent flashes racing along the highway, closing in on you.

The lights make you sick, yet you can't stop staring.

The cop car is moving along, closer, closer, closer.

Money-sniffing dogs looking to take you down.

And then, silently, glides past without stopping. You feel the air rush out of your body, steadying yourself.

Did that really just happen?

Same car, or different?

Just another scene in the sick dance that plays with your head. You tell yourself that it's a coincidence, just a cop onto something else. If they were onto you they would have popped red and blue the second you pulled away.

At least that's what you tell yourself.

Just another reminder they've got their nets out for the hundreds of black, lonely miles between this chunk of desert and Bobby B. Basically, Jet, there's no way you make it to Santa Monica.

Abort mission and thumb your way back to Phoenix.

There's no cover, just clumps of knee-high desert. You're watching the highway and waiting for the next set of headlights to cut black morning. Or maybe that cop coming back this way. Nothing.

You watch one more car approach, wondering, praying, then breathing easier as it passes, just two red taillights now glowing in the desert night. Another 60-second box you can check.

Straight ahead is the only way to freedom.

Back on the highway, 14 miles later, ghosting through a little elevation rise where the terrain changes from flat scrubland to rocky hills with long, spidery ocotillo branches fingering sky. When you pass the turnoff for Highway 60 to Wickenburg and Prescott, you know you're closing in on the California border. You squeeze leather and breathe deep.

Traffic's sparse, and right now you're in a wide gap all by yourself, a set of headlights way behind you that hasn't gained any ground. You take a deep breath and a sip of Diet Coke. You're about to pass the point of no return.

Cross the state line, and your crime becomes a federal charge. Absolute worst part of the trip.

More than two hours in, fruit-patrol dudes looking to take you down. Most times they just hand you a tourist map and wave you through. Sometimes they ask if you have any fruits or vegetables. Sometimes you blow through and no one's even manning the booth. Rolle told you they're looking for pests that wipe out crops, not stolen cars, but the whole process of being asked questions by people in uniform, while sitting in a $115,000 car you do not own, is unbearable. You make the silent promise, never again, not as long as you live.

You pass the two exits for Quartzsite, then mile marker 5 and that last rest area you never stop at anymore. When the speed limit drops to 65, your heart races because you're less than five minutes away now.

Stub Marlboro.

Check the rearview: two trucks and a gray sedan.

Speed limit drops to 55.

Sign: State Line Upcoming, Inspection Station 1 Mile.

Speed limit keeps dropping.

45.

35.

Another sign: Inspection Station 1/4 mile.

Here comes another 60-second block. Always thinking, is the one where it ends? Or do you get to check off one more box?

Two cars ahead of you in this lane.

When you can see the border, your heart really starts thumping: a rounded adobe structure over the road with a bell on top and four individual bays through which you can pass. The lettering stretches all the way across the structure: California Agriculture Station. Now there's only one car in front of you.

Cross the California state line.

Nice man asks if you have any oranges or stolen $115,000 imports today.

This is it, all or nothing, your entire life squeezed into the next few seconds. Inches and seconds, Bobby B always says, are what separate those who drop clean and the ones sitting in prison right now.

Inches and seconds.

The nice man in the uniform waves you forward. You swear he knows something's up, but of course he doesn't. Then again, how obvious is this screaming yellow car? How obvious is your guilty face? It's all over. No, it's not, Jet, shut up.

Everyone just shut up and chill.

Brain silence.

Good.

You tighten your grip on the steering wheel, take a deep breath, and pull forward. You've already dropped the window halfway. Just as you pull up, the man in uniform holds up his hand for you to stop. "Wait," he says, walking over and talking to another uniformed man in the next booth.

Heart rate jumps 20 notches, echoing in your head now.

What's this?

Straight ahead you can see the sign: Welcome to California. Entering Pacific Time.

Except you're stuck over here in Mountain Time in a stolen Porsche 911 Turbo. You'll never get to Pacific Time. Maybe punch the accelerator and disappear into California morning before he comes back. Probably wouldn't even remember you sitting here. Then again, the driver of that empty California Highway Patrol car over there might take an interest. Could that be him? The car you saw glide by flashing red and blue?

Your brain is all, just wait it out, stay calm, be cool. They don't know the car is stolen. Oh God, this is bad.

Pretty much going crazy now.

Whole world knows you're guilty. Roll video, you're on the next Cops special, Babes Gone Bad edition. Check your local listings.

Get out of here now. Make your break.

Probably that white car you outran back there radioed ahead to the car sitting there. He's in that booth drinking lukewarm coffee right now, waiting for you to tangle yourself in his net and then laugh when you're swept up.

Just when you think your brain's going to redline, you see both uniformed men walking back this way, something in the hand of the one who told you to wait here. You close your eyes and breathe. The next few seconds... Months. Years. At life's end.

Everything played. Menopaused and rocking-chaired, shrivelled and gray-haired, wondering why you did all those things and wasted all those years in prison. Could never vote again: felony charge times ten.

Flashes in your head like popping fluorescent tubes. Then you open your eyes.

Decision time.

You ready?

Ready for what?

You glance back over at the patrol car, still no driver, then back at the two men who are about to take away your new life. Your foot instinctively pushes the accelerator.

Thundering mass surges.

Tach sweeping hard right.

Stay or go?

The question pistons through your head a hundred times in the flash of a second— stay or go?— but you do nothing. The man slides your death certificate through the gap in the window and says something. You take the paper and shake your head, things moving in underwater motion now. So this is how it all ends, four hours away from freedom, Jet times one snagged by the fruit police with the purple light just starting to crack the black all around you.

The desert highway beat you down to nothing, not even a spirited chase, and won. The sound of steel ratchets on wrists, smell the back of a sweat-grubbed patrol car, a ratty Crown Vic bench seat mealy and yellowed with tears and the agony of broken promises.

Chapter Fourteen

DALE GOT YOU HALFWAY TO QUITTING. Your own little voice, when you finally started listening, took you all the way. Day after you go to clean out your locker.

At coffee, Dale says your decisions are not about right and wrong, or good and evil, and he goes, Oscar Wilde said the same thing about books, no such thing as a moral or immoral book. Books are well written or they are badly written.

You sort of get it.

He goes, the correct path is about seeing all the layers of the universe simultaneously and not making any judgments either way. Dale doesn't even smoke weed to come up with stuff like that. Simply see what invites pain and confusion into your life and then stop inviting.

Yeah, but what about the money? And rent and food.

Awareness.

And what about how your asshole father left you, and the way Mom acts like you don't even exist? You're just a kid, really, so what are you supposed to do?

CHAPTER FOURTEEN

Awareness.

And so you stop. After you clean out your locker and pack up your stuff, Alex hands you an envelope. The return address says *Miller Foster Home for Boys*. It doesn't register until you open the envelope that it's from the 15-year-old ZigZag, the cute, lanky kid who connected you to Dale in the first place.

You met the kid coming out of the restaurant run by that sleaze the Toad. ZigZag scared the crap out of you the way he came right up behind you in the dark. Tall black kid, two in the morning, deserted parking lot in a blown-out part of town. You almost pepper-spray him. You find out quick enough, though, that he's just a little mental, but not dangerous, and completely adorable. Only family he has is his dad, who's in jail for beating up some female undercover cop. Maybe that's where you connect: welcome to the LDC, the Lost Dads Club. The kid's definitely off a little, but right from that moment he's like the little brother you never had.

You take him to the Waffle Shack and the kid inhales two plates of strawberry waffles with whipped cream. He totally makes you laugh. Big, curious eyes. Then you drop him off at the hospital where his volunteer Big Brother is laid up with testicular cancer. You give him $100 before he gets out of the car.

Awareness.

If you aren't hooking up with the filthy pig Toad for cash, you don't take ZigZag out for waffles. If you don't take ZigZag out for waffles, you don't meet Dale. If you don't meet Dale, maybe you're still spinning your wheels in the mud.

You pull out the single sheet of paper in the envelope. Handwritten in thick black ink is a poem called 'the pramis' by ZigZag. You smile.

Last time you saw him is seven months before you start boosting cars. Against your better judgment, his Big Brother talks you into helping them get some loot ZigZag stole back into the safe at the restaurant. Of course you do it, like a bad cliché. Fallen angel with a heart of gold. Whatever. You're no cliché; you're flesh and blood.

You're not a normal person.

That night, after the big drama, you wait in the parking lot and drive ZigZag back to the hospital when he gets off work. You also make plans to meet Dale later for drinks in what turns out to be your first time together. The kid's Big

Brother, this dude Dean Singer everyone just calls Singer, is in really bad shape. ZigZag doesn't really understand what's happening. He just goes on and on about the plan Dale concocted to put the money back and how everything went that night, but Singer's pretty gone, sort of nodding in and out. The last thing ZigZag says to his Big Brother is how you kissed ZigZag right on the lips when he came out of the restaurant. Singer manages a smile for the first time.

Few minutes later, when you and ZigZag come back from walking down the hall to get a couple sodas, there are two nurses in the room that weren't there before. They never say a word. ZigZag doesn't understand why they have the white sheet pulled over Singer's head. You pull ZigZag aside and hug him and try to explain. Can't find the right words. ZigZag moves toward the bed and pulls the sheet down and strokes his friend's face with his hand, telling him to be happy because finally they're unhooking all those damn machines, and now he can just go back to being Singer the way he always was. No more noise, he says.

TWELVE-THIRTY p.m., 31,000 feet, somewhere over the Arizona desert. You order a third beer from the flight attendant. You have an entire row to yourself, thank God, forehead pressed flat against the cold plastic window.

Sex is power.

Mom tells you this that same day you get your first period.

Relationships always crack up in the end, so you'd better get out while the getting's still good.

Mom tells you this two years ago as she's sliding off the deep end with booze. Full quart of vodka a day. She tells you she's going to live with her boyfriend in Atlantic City. By "boyfriend" she really means greasy loser.

She says you should come along, make a new start.

Thanks, Mom, but Atlantic City is not your idea of a new start, especially with her jobless wonder of a man. Then you lock yourself in your bedroom and cry. While Mom's at least around, sort of, Dad's just become this big ghost question mark. Last time you saw him was three years ago. Dad gives you 45 minutes of his time at an Italian restaurant, and half of that he's reading some thick government report. Dad's the one gave you the cartoon name. You decide halfway through your linguine he's not the one. You're putting your money on possible Dutch Dad #1 or #2. Bump your odds to 50/50. *A coin flip.*

Your entire existence is a coin flip.

But there's one problem: There's virtually no way to track down either of these two footnotes* (*may be Jenna's father) since Mom can't remember last names.

With Mom gone, you think having the apartment all to yourself is the greatest thing ever, total freedom. But to keep up with the bills you have to work two jobs, fast food by day and 24-hour diner by night. Paying bills is not as great as you thought it would be.

Meanwhile, your girlfriends are doing other things, most legal and some not. You consider these legal options. You even go with Jordan one night to the topless bar where she works, a place called The Monkey Club. The place is gross, no way you're doing that. Jordan takes you backstage, and you hang out in the dressing room while she puts on her makeup. You can't believe how many girls work at a place called The Monkey Club. Some friendly, some not, all with this far-off look in their eyes. Not because they don't like you, Jordan says, or because of the coke or meth or Valium, take your pick, but because you just learn to check out to get through the long night of bouncing your tits for strangers. She says mostly all you think about during is getting your feet out of the stiletto heels and back onto flat ground. She says you can take a grand off a guy and not remember his name five minutes after he walks out.

The owner of the place, this guy Cadillac Tom, comes in the room and gives this lame little pep talk. You don't know why, but as soon as you see him you feel sorry for him. He's got that same glassy look in his eyes. Light Hispanic, not bad-looking except for a narrow little moustache that's sort of creepy. He's lean and compact, like he runs seven miles a day. He wears his orange silk shirt buttoned up all the way to his neck. Jordan says one night he drank too many martinis and told her his dream as a little boy was to play shortstop for the Yankees. Now he comes here every night and listens to the games on radio in his office while girls take off their shirts to pay his rent on some gross fifth-floor walk-up.

Back onto flat ground.

He tells the dancers not to forget about the *Monkey Club* T-shirts— he holds one up— and to push bottles of champagne. Cadillac Tom also says to watch the touching because the liquor board has been around again busting his balls. During his five-minute talk, only one or two of the dancers look up from doing their makeup. When he's finished talking he stares at you for a few seconds and walks over with the black T-shirts draped over his right shoulder. He never breaks eye contact when he says, "Who's the babe, Jordan?"

Jordan's curling her eyelashes. "Cadillac, Jenna. Jenna, Cadillac. But she goes by her last name: 'Jet.' Isn't that cool?"

He rubs his hands together and nods. "Jet. Pleasure."

So far, you don't share his sentiment.

"You dance?"

"No," Jordan says, looking at you and Cadillac in her mirror, "Put your tongue back in your mouth and leave her alone."

"Do I get any respect around here?" he asks you, taking a step back and tipping his head sideways to totally check you out. Jordan rolls her eyes and leans back toward the mirror. Cadillac Tom pulls a business card out of his back pocket and takes a pen off Jordan's vanity. "I'm giving you my direct number. Rings right in the office."

"Oooh, rings in the office," Jordan says.

"Am I talking to you?"

"Whatever."

He writes on the back, looks up, and smiles when he hands you the card. "You start dancing, you come here first. Promise me."

"Yeah, promise nothing," Jordan says. "She's just chilling."

"I'm serious. Tell her, Jordan: There's nowhere to be but here."

Jordan rolls her eyes again and shakes her head. "Oh yeah. This place is right behind 'FedEx' and 'Hewlett-Packard' on the premier employer ranking. I got two words for you: health insurance."

"Yeah? Well I got one for you: amortization. As in, like, you want to pay the note on this building every month, and then we'll talk health insurance?"

"See what I gotta put up with just to make rent," Jordan says while she uncaps a tube of burgundy lipstick.

A few days after, she tells you she left that night with $600 cash stuffed in her purse. It took her five hours to make six bills. It takes you two weeks to earn that much in tips at the diner. Maybe it's time to consider a career change. But then all you can think about is how once you cross that line, can you ever go back?

You keep grinding out your around-the-clock restaurant schedule. Even busting out 24/7, it only takes six months for your landlord to tack the notice on your door. Although you pay your rent on time every month (barely), you don't realize Mom still owed four months' back rent. So the landlord wants it all: back rent *plus* the current month, or you're out. Rent times five in one chunk.

Like, what's the landlord think you are, a millionaire?

When you call Mom to ask her to send what she owes, she apologizes and says she'll talk to the boyfriend and call you back. Three days later, nothing. When you finally get her again she apologizes some more and says she hasn't had a chance to ask him, but she will and let you know. Then she changes the subject and says why don't you come to Atlantic City for a couple days to unwind.

Unwind? You're about to become homeless and she wants you to come unwind. All you can think is, time to start your new life, as far from here as possible. You hang up and cry. You're officially evicted three days later, totally embarrassing, and the landlord says she's getting a lawyer to file an injunction against you for all the back rent plus interest, blah, blah, blah.

You tell her you paid all your rent and anything before that is on your mom, but the landlord doesn't want to hear it. The debt's on you now, she keeps saying.

Jordan and her friend Tina, who share a tiny one-bedroom next to the intersection of two freeways, say you can stay with them. They share the only bedroom, which puts you on the floor (they've been saying for months they need to go buy a couch). They're not lesbians, but they share a king-size bed because that's what they have. From Day One you feel like you're crashing someone else's party.

Their apartment is better than the rathole you left, which is kind of like saying dying by lethal injection is better than a hanging. The freeway noise is bad, but eventually it's like this constant roaring sound you don't really notice. You have ongoing nightmares about the three-inch roach you pull from your cheek at 3 a.m. But it's free and, temporarily, it's home.

Jordan and Tina are vampires. Never up before one or two in the afternoon, and then stay in all day—paint their nails, give each other pedicures, do their hair, watch talk shows, do bong hits, maybe a little blow. Then when it gets dark, they venture out to make money. Jordan and Tina teach you everything you never wanted to know about ugly ways to make money.

They tell you with your face, your body, you can pull $2,000 a day easy. Look at them, they go, they're dogs compared to you, and they're in tall cotton. You didn't know Jordan also works at a place called Angel Escorts, this nothing place in a strip mall where all the other suites have VACANT signs on the dirty door. They introduce you to their boss, Alex, a girl.

Nothing against them, but you feel sick even being there. You think again about crossing the line and getting stuck on that other side like them. Next thing, you're living at the intersection of two freeways and need a bong hit and a white rail to wake up at 2 p.m. Then what?

Here's how the gig works.

The goal is to extract as much money as possible from each client without really doing anything. Like an extended tease that never pays off. They all laugh.

You don't really get it.

That means $150 flat to show up at their door. "Hello, $150 please." You split that with the agency. Anything else the client wants after that is between you and him on a tip basis, 20 points back to the agency. Any sexual contact with clients is illegal. But it's not illegal to charge $500 to go to lunch. Or $1,000 to do a striptease dance. Or $2,000 for an out-of-town trip to attend some boring conference in a low-cut dress that shows off your cleavage.

No sex?

Alex goes, absolutely not. What happens between you and the client is private. They all laugh again. Supply and demand determine market price. Did you know working girls are statistically safer and cleaner than the general population?

Statistically safer and cleaner?

All you want to do is get out of there as fast as you can. Get back to your bathroom at the tiny one-bedroom, the only place private, where you can run the shower and cry without anyone hearing.

You hold out another five months, and when you're not passed out from exhaustion on your floor you look for a decent job. But every ad and every interview leads you back to a sad truth: you make more per hour waiting tables. But still not enough to have your own apartment. How does anyone get out of this loop?

You call your mom again and ask for help. She never really says no, but she changes the subject and starts talking about a bunch of crap you don't care about, like where they spent the weekend and how she's really happy with the greasy loser.

Whatever.

You're back at Angel Escorts talking to Alex, telling her just a few months, enough to clean up Mom's mess (you suspect that landlord will make the rest of your life hell if you don't pay her back) and then just a little extra to start your new life.

No sex, you go. Right?

Right, she says, smiling and then laughing again. You just stick with me.

Chapter Fifteen

"YOU NEED TO PULL OVER?"

Nothing. So the nice man asks again, "Ma'am, you need to pull over?"

State line crossing. So that's it, Jet, you're just going to let these two haul you in without a fight? Even with your ass wrapped in leather and Stuttgart steel. Except I-10 west from here takes you into more endless desert, the only Speed Yellow Porsche for 100 square. You're a Day-Glo bullseye on black velvet. Might as well be in an orange rubber raft in a brown field.

"A map."

Your brain's all, huh?

"A map? So you don't get lost." Then he smiles as the other one says, "Yeah, we wouldn't want you to get lost."

He points at the paper in your hand, and for the first time you look down at what you're holding: California Travel Ideas Map.

A stupid tourist map.

You have to think it again: a tourist map.

You look up and smile. If they didn't suspect anything before, they probably do now. Like a moron, all you say is, "This is a nice one."

They're both smiling, then the first one says, "Enjoy your stay."

You nod. "Thanks. Thank you."

And with that you thumb-shift your way onto California turf in a stolen Porsche 911. Thirty seconds that felt like three days and aged you 30 years. Normal twenty-something girls don't commit felony crime number ten before breakfast.

Holy shit. You're in California!

This part of the bleak desert is definitely not palm trees, Hollywood and neon green bikinis. You think about how much time you have left.

Four more hours.

Four more hours, and then a lifetime of freedom.

Time is for you, time is against you.

Awareness.

Then it hits you in a bright flash that this is all so wonderfully crazy, it just might work. Then again, don't get cocky this early. Four more hours is a lifetime out here.

White lines.

Black desert.

Engine rumbling.

Time is for you, time is against you.

Chapter Sixteen

HARRISON WEST.

First time you hear that name you think muscles, moustache and a man-part the size of a baby's arm. So much for names. Harrison West is some kind of engineer heading out to California to study earthquakes or something. A graduate teaching assistant who's all brain, no brawn. He's maybe a "5" in bad light, after a couple drinks, and then one more. But more important, Harrison West is your free ticket to a new life.

Maybe Mom's right, that sex is power (or even the remote specter of sex), because Harrison is willing to drive you across the country even when you tell him flat out, direct as you can be, no way, no funny business, two rooms at every hotel, you're not that kind of girl, etc. Even so, he's checking you out anyway and as his mouth goes "no problem" his brain is all, "Please, Lord, let me hit that."

You rush around grabbing clothes and make two calls and then one almost-call. First Dale. You try to leave a message telling him everything you want to say, but you start crying and end up sounding stupid and just say you'll call him again later after you get settled in California. Then you call the landlord and tell her about the cashier's check you already put in the mail, full back rent plus 10 percent for her trouble, and apologize again. Trying to do the right thing here and all that. The almost-call is to your mother, but you hang up while it's ringing. What more is there to say? She said everything she's going to say when she moved to Atlantic City with the greaser and left you here with back rent.

Awareness.

Then you sit and wait for Harrison. You think again about calling Mom to say goodbye. You sort of miss her already and don't want to ever see her again, all at the same time. Weird. Cold sheets of rain are slapping the windows. California sunshine only 3,000 miles away.

Harrison West rolls up in a black Chevy Camaro with bad rust around the wheel wells and a back bumper that won't make it to the Mississippi River. You stuff your duffel bag in the back seat. The windshield wipers squeak each time on the down stroke. The car smells sweet because Harrison picked you up a cinnamon roll big enough to feed a family of five. You thank him and start to eat it and then start crying as he pulls away from the curb. What a mental patient. It's all hitting you, how your mom's a drunk living with some loser young enough to be your brother, Atlantic City, and your dad just some ghost who haunts your dreams. Now you wish you'd called Mom.

Four days later, you roll into Phoenix to visit one of Harrison West's friends, a guy named Reginald Rolle but everyone just calls him Rolle. They seem an odd match: Rolle's super-athletic, good looking and into cars, weed and the music of Johnny Cash. Harrison's pretty much not any of those, and he's into earthquakes and seismic retrofitting of buildings. But Harrison grew up in Phoenix where they played high school football together.

Meeting Rolle is not an original component of your overall *West Coast or Bust* campaign. It just came up as more of a strategic troop adjustment conceived in the heat of battle. That first night, you get up to go to the bathroom, middle of the night, and the idea hits you as you sit on the toilet peeing. Minutes later, you accidentally-on-purpose end up in Rolle's bed. No sex or anything like that, just that safe feeling to be wrapped up in his arms. He doesn't seem all that surprised to wake up with you there, and he doesn't say anything. Just hugs you like you've been his girlfriend for years and goes back to sleep.

This is the first normal encounter you've had in nine months. Normal is not having to negotiate a price and count money up front. Normal is not going to dinner with someone old enough to be your grandfather. Normal is not driving to see the Toad with that sick, lonely pain all around you.

Snuggling with Rolle, you feel normal.

This isn't the start of your new life, but it's definitely the prologue.

September in Arizona.

Hot days, hot nights.

Next morning Rolle says you can hang with him a week or two, no hurry, he has you covered. He's super-sweet and has pretty much the most amazing body you've ever seen. Harrison West is all, OK, later, and then it's just you and Rolle. It's like being on vacation. You spend your nights with him, nothing beyond second base, and your days by the pool browning up your white skin.

Rolle keeps telling you to take your time, no hurry, no need to rush off to California. Besides, he makes pretty good money between Meryl Mack's and the side deals he always has going. You ask about the boxed computers he's selling out of the apartment, which he tells you his uncle liquidated when his electronics store went out of business. You're not really buying that one, but he turns a nice chunk of change and gives you $1,000 cash to buy clothes. Meanwhile, Rolle never stops talking about his plan to open his own shop because he's sick of Meryl Mack's.

You think about your mom.

Quart of vodka a day in Atlantic City.

Then one day Rolle just goes, check this out, there's this Irish dude out in L.A. called Billy B who promised this other guy Rolle knows they could be shitting in tall grass inside of a week. The guy just got out and doesn't want to risk his parole, but if Rolle could find a female runner, someone to move merchandise from Phoenix to LA, man that would be rad.

Here's what Rolle says after you both do bong hits: three weeks, ten cars at $15,000 each, 60/40 split. This is where you're supposed to tell Rolle he's crazy. Wave it off and laugh. But you know the gig well, all or nothing. A sick comfort in walking to the edge just to see if you fall off. The cartoon name, the three words trapped in your head for as long as you can remember.

Chapter Seventeen

SCENE OF THE CRIME(S).

Says how you end up out here, rolling west past the sign that says Blythe City Limits, an ugly hurt working your stomach stronger than you expected. Kill zone. Money-sniffing dogs looking to take you down. Whine of German metal cutting black air. Porsche Tiptronic S. Thumb-shift to Fourth to grab RPMs and pass an 18-wheel cattle truck. Pink snouts nosed through trailer holes.

Heart rate and sweaty palms. Hard lump rising:

Highway Patrol, Next Exit

Once you cross into California, the speed limit drops from 75 to 70, so you've adjusted the cruise control down five. Once you're out of Blythe, this stretch of I-10 is really ugly. Right lane deep-grooved by the 18-wheelers, jacking the car around in unsettled swerves. You pass a sign that says you're 43 miles from Desert Center and 219 miles from LA, which means you're right in the heart of the devil's playground.

Checking the rearview.

Just one big rig. Black desert closing in. Then a quick flash of comic relief each time.
"Here it comes," you say.

State Prison
Do not stop for hitchhikers

You remember seeing this sign on number one, thinking, yeah, good idea, thanks for the warning. "Now watch," you say, laughing. Now you're passing the second sign:

Rest Area
Next Exit

Some kind of sick joke. Whatever you do, don't pick up that dude hitchhiking in chains and striped pajamas, but look, let's stop here and picnic. You listen to the engine hum, Porsche lurching left and right in the rounded grooves.

Awareness.

You ever think maybe Dad really did love you and want to be with you, and it was Mom who drove him away? Made up that whole story about he was the one sent you away. Turned it into you and her against him. You're not sure where this possibility comes from or why it popped into your head here of all places. But there it is. You let it sit there for a few miles.

OK, maybe there's a way you can get in touch with him in Beirut. Maybe he'd fly you to Europe. Maybe that's part of your new life. Maybe. Except everything hinges on getting this car to LA and Jet times one back to Phoenix.

Inches and seconds.

That's the only difference between Europe and reconciliation versus straight to the hot squat, striped pajamas and permanent Snack Pak for some bull dyke with a goatee.

Three hours in, you pass the exit for Desert Center and breathe a choked bit of relief. Another mini-milestone. The car's running like a six-figure ride should.

Clockwork.

You're weaving through the gauntlet, no signs of trouble. Daylight now instead of dark. Probably isn't any safer, but daylight feels so much safer than black desert. Either way, still rolling west.

Maybe, just maybe.

All the way to Santa Monica.

You're passing the halfway point, these weird rings of burned-out palm trees out in the middle of nowhere like some alien planted them for kicks. A sign: SPEED ENFORCED BY AIRCRAFT. When you run stolen cars, words on signs take on heightened significance.

Enforced.

Speed.

Highway Patrol.

State prison.

Wouldn't surprise you to see a sign that says:

deep wicked freaky
Your ass is ours.

Chapter Eighteen

PHOENIX.

Rolle trying to be funny on the way home from Sky Harbor Airport: "See, hanging with a babe got a cartoon name, your brain gets sneaky, starts slipping you new ones while you sleep. See what I'm saying?"

Your head hurts too much to even guess. The beer buzz is gone, and now all you can think about is sleep.

"Like this morning, baby. One popped into my head so loud woke me up. Tried to just go back to sleep, but when the inspiration knocks on your brain when you're face-down? You best take it seriously."

You turn away: headed west through the baked, brown desolation of another thousand-degree September day. Not a cloud in sight, just that rarefied blue you never thought you'd wish away. Clouds, rain, hello?

"So I wrote down the new name, Whack Savage, and tried to go back to sleep, except as soon as you open the gate, it's like a damn free-for-all in your head. So up comes another one: Superfly Pinstripe. So what you think, baby?"

Four months of your life.

"Now Whack Savage, maybe a dude got a knife between his teeth and muscles all popping off. But then again, Superfly Pinstripe, that's tight, the whole erotic crossover thing. Both of them are right up in your face, you know, but you want the mystery, too. Good name has to make people wonder what a brother's all about."

Hot, tired. Burned down to nothing. Head throb. "Seriously, what are you even talking about?"

"Ain't you been listening? The new shop? Damn, girl, that's what I been telling you the last five minutes."

Three weeks.

Six hours at a time.

You drive the finest cars in the world: fast, sleek and precise. Now you're in Rolle's 70-something GMC van, dented all around where he and his friends always start kicking after too many beers. A *black* van in Phoenix. That's like living on the sun and owning nothing but gasoline slippers. Even more fatal is the air conditioner that blows a faint trail of lukewarm air, which almost seems worse than no AC because at least then you could roll down the windows and stop the charade. This way, you just sit helplessly and slowly roast in this mobile oven. You want that original or extra crispy?

Every time you get in the van you immediately start fiddling with the knobs and adjusting vents in a vain search for cold air. You know it's futile, but playing with the knobs at least makes you feel like you might elicit something cold. Supposedly Rolle bought the van from a guy in Dallas who says he bought it from Dan Reeves who Rolle says was an assistant coach under Dallas Cowboys head coach Tom Landry back in the '70s. What? And yeah, that's why Rolle calls his van *America's Ride*.

"So you think either those got potential?"

"Either what?" Rolle's face is glistened.

"I'm thinking Superfly Pinstripe, get a bad-ass brother with a can of spray paint in the logo there somehow. Big 'ol gold hoops in both ears. Check this: He's wearing a necklace says SUPERFLY, and he's spraying out PINSTRIPE. You see it coming alive right out the can."

The heat's compressing your head, patience and diplomacy obliterated in a hot swirl of desert dust. "I was going to wait to say this, but whatever,

I'm just going to say it: We have to divvy up the money now. I'm not doing another car."

Rolle gives you a look like you just told him that before Phoenix, back east, you used to be a man, that you were trouser packing Big Jim and the twins. "Say what, baby?"

"Our money. This fifteen," you hold up your purse, "plus what we have in the safe-deposit box. That's it; we're done."

"Meaning what?"

"Meaning nothing. Meaning we're done. No more. I'm not going out there again. Let's go to the first bank right now and get the key. Then I'll take you to the money."

"Baby, why you clowning? What'd we agree? We each get our cut when we finish all ten."

"Ten. Why ten? Why that random number anyway, I mean, it's greedy. We're going to get busted. This is so stupid. I'm not even like this, like, I'm stealing cars? What is that?" You look to the blazing desert sky for a response.

"You ain't stealing cars, baby, you just driving them. Big difference."

"I messed it all up again. I had my chance to start over, and I messed it all up."

"You ain't mess up nothing, baby, we doing great. Soon we'll both be macking it hard. Don't be messing with the plan now. An agreement's an agreement. You know you walk you get nothing like we said."

"Fine."

"Fine then."

"Then you get nothing, too."

"Fine."

"Fine."

Silence. Eventually he says, "You want to walk away from a phat stack of cash? This is some seriously easy money, girl."

Easy money.

Barter it.

Sell it.

Give it away.

"We make a good team. Why you going all menstrual on me anyway?"

"What?"

"You get all tense and say shit you don't really mean. It's cool, I got you."

You want to scream.

"We need to stop at Circle K?" he asks.

"What?"

"You know."

"No, I don't know. Enlighten me."

"You need some hygiene products? Female stuff?"

"Rolle…" You're speechless. Why do they always think it's that?

"It's cool, baby. I think I saw some of that stuff under the sink a few days ago. Both kinds, the little bullet ones and them diaper pads."

It's not worth it. You just need sleep. Face-down for 12 hours with the AC cranked to meat locker. You know he's not going to divvy up until you get the last $15,000. He needs the full $50,000 and then some to open his shop. Only problem is neither of you can get the money without the other one. Worst part, you're the genius who came up with the way to make that happen.

Double-Blind, Two-Box Lock-Up.

Your idea, Rolle's clever title.

Two people. One pair dark sunglasses and one walking stick. Two safe-deposit boxes at two different banks. At first, Rolle is all, huh? After he gets it, he gives it the name.

You ask, why does it need a name?

Because, he says, it's the tightest setup he's ever heard, smiling big, how all this time he had no idea he's been dining at the "Y" of a genius. That's how compliments from Rolle go: bittersweet.

Here's how the gig works.

The day you land back in Phoenix with the cash from number one, Rolle picks you up at Sky Harbor in the mobile kiln. Early September in most places means maybe some falling leaves, summer's wane. A cloud, perhaps. In Phoenix it means another month of the same red-hot radiation you've endured since May, 100-plus daily.

With the van spitting its faint stream of AC at the airport curb, you and Rolle switch seats. You tell him not to get stoned for this, but he's hitting a fat spliff anyway while you put the bandages on him and eye-patch his vision into total oblivion. You sit back and look at your work, white patches over both his eyes. Then you slip the wrap-around sunglasses on him.

"Can you see?"

"Can't see shit."

"Promise?"

"Darker than a motherfucker in here." He sticks both his arms out and feels his way through the air until his left hand finds your right shoulder, then starting to move down toward your boob.

"Whatever." You push his hand away and, before slipping the steering column shift lever to Drive, fiddle with the AC vents and hold up your hand just in case. Nothing but a faint wisp against your palm. "Can't you get this AC recharged or something?"

Rolle has his head tipped back against the seat while he takes a hit off the joint pinched between his fingers. Besides the sunglasses, all he has on are Guess overalls (no shirt) and black DKNY slip-on shoes. Rolle doesn't own a single pair of underwear, and he claims, not counting diapers, he's never worn underwear in his life. He doesn't lift his head to talk. "Baby, how many times we go through this? This here's '70s Detroit metal, and ain't no Detroit brother needs big-time AC in the '70s."

"What's the year have to do with anything? They still had summer back then." You pull away from the curb and cut all the way across to the left lane in one swoop, someone honking, then onto the main exit road from the airport.

"Global warming."

You glance over at him. "Global warming?"

"Hell yeah. Brothers back then was just chillin' 24/7, even in summer. Weather's buggin' now, baby. Global warming's got everything all discombobulatory. Vehicles today require a totally new level of heating, refrigeration and all-around weather-proofing technology. Back then? All a brother needed was a straight-block eight and curb feelers."

You look over again as he hits the hydro. Somehow he just blamed his van's shitty AC on global weather patterns. You smile. Rolle could get a white-sheeted Grand Wizard to scrub his toilet and grill him up a filet mignon.

Twenty minutes later, at the first bank, you give Rolle his cane and your arm and lead him into the customer service waiting area. You open a safe-deposit box here in Rolle's name with him blindfolded. You tell the bank lady he just had eye surgery for glaucoma. Doctor said he might never see again. The bank lady doesn't ask any more questions.

Once inside the safe, Rolle peels off one patch and watches $15,000 go in the box and get locked away. You hold the key, repatch his eye, lead him out and drive away. Then after numerous turns and cut-backs to make sure he has no clue where the money is iced, you pull over and reverse the procedure. Now you're the blind passenger. Patches and dark glasses.

Rolle chooses bank #2, leads you in, and you open a second safe-deposit box in your name. He tells the bank lady you got battery acid splashed in your eyes at a monster truck rally. Fried your eyeballs right out the sockets. Damn shame, just two red holes up in your head now. The bank lady doesn't ask any more questions.

Once inside the safe, you peel off one patch, put the key to safe-deposit box #1 in the box and lock it away. You get to hold the key to box #2. You repatch the eye, Rolle leads you out and drives around a while before he lets you pull off the patches.

Each time you come back from LA $15,000 to the good, you and Rolle repeat the process to keep the money iced. You know where the cash is stashed at bank #1. He knows where the money key is stashed at bank #2. You hold the key to get the money key. Neither can wade into tall cotton without the other.

Double-Blind, Two-Box Lock-Up.

Chapter Nineteen

ELEVEN MILES OUTSIDE COACHELLA.

Thirteen to Indio, just over two hours to LA. You've got some serious sit-down business, bladder about to pop.

Rule #1 No speeding.

Rule #2 Avoid stopping. Being parked is dangerous to your health. Stopping will get you popped faster than this car can hit 60. But short of trying to go in a cup or squatting in the desert, there's not much you can do here. That means you're going to have to park this $115,000 rig in Indio, California.

Population 43,780.

Current percentage of Porsche 911 Turbos owned by residents: zero-point-zero. This makes you very nervous.

You roll through the nothing town five below the limit and pull into the first convenience store you see. You park on the far right to put three empty spaces between the Porsche and the sprawling white Dodge truck with dualies. You kill the engine.

Standstill in Indio, clock running.

Next 60-second block underway.

OK, need to make this fast. The leather seats make that sound that only leather makes as you climb out, "Carrera" spelled out in cursive script on the doorjamb.

Standstill in Indio, clock running.

A man coming out with a tall plastic traveler mug and a gooey-looking donut backs out the door and stops to hold it open. "Morning," he says, smiling. Must be the driver of the big Dodge, pretty old, probably 40s, big gut and black, thick-rimmed glasses. You smile back.

"Morning."

Standstill in Indio, clock running.

You look around the quiet parking lot. Nothing but the big Dodge and furiously fast Porsche. Quiet is good, but quiet also makes your palms sweaty. Something brewing out there. Calm before the storm.

You got the game to keep it together and stay cool?

"Looks like you're traveling in style. That yours?"

The car. Always with the car. "Boyfriend's, actually."

"That's a nice one. Turbo, right? You can tell by the red disc brakes. Air scoops behind both doors." *He's pointing with the donut, impressed with his automotive acumen.*

You nod. "Yeah, I guess." *Here we go.*

"Boyfriend must love you an awful lot."

"Oh yeah. Anyway, nice talking to you."

"Oh yeah, go right ahead. I'll keep an eye on your car 'til you get back."

Shit. "Great. Thanks."

Inside the store, bathroom, thick stream, relief, wipe, zip, go.

Out in the store, smile at the clerk, chunky white guy with his red hair pulled back into a ponytail and a thick goatee. You wander the aisles to kill a couple 60-second blocks in hopes the guy outside will leave.

"Nice ride," *the clerk says, sipping from a steaming cup.*

The car again. Does it ever stop?

"Yours?"

"Fiancé's, actually."

You're standing in the aisle and looking at him over a row of Fritos bags. This is why Rule #2: too much attention in these cars. Everyone wants to ask you about the car. Everyone wants to impress you with how much they know about the car. Everyone wants to share some story about a guy they knew who knew a guy who had one of those and here's what happened one time coming off a light, and on and on.

"Cousin has a '68 Camaro Super Sport with a 396, four-speed. Got the posi-rear. Rally wheels. Car kicks tail."

Does any of this mean anything to you?

Even worse, they really think they have a chance against a machine clocked at 185, according to Rolle, on the test track at Weissach.

"Cousin's Camaro's got kick-ass horsepower. You know much about cars?"

No, not really, but why not? After all, he started it. "A little," *you say, nodding and grabbing the biggest bag of Doritos Nacho Cheese chips. A fun way to kill another 60 seconds and not think about how sick to your stomach you are with that guy waiting out by his truck. Is he just a small-town nobody with nothing better to do, or does he pose a threat? Undercover? Brother of a cop? Headhunter? You walk up and put the chips on the counter. Let him have it, Jet.*

"That's a limited-production Porsche 911 Turbo. All-wheel drive. Twin turbochargers and a water-cooled, horizontally opposed flat six. Four hundred and twenty ponies, but stroke and bore the cylinders you can take it up to 500. Zero to 60 in four-point-two and back to standstill in two-point-six. And believe me, you will stop on a buffalo nickel because it's got internally vented, cross-drilled brakes."

"Damn," *he says, shaking his head.* "How you know all that?"

"I don't really. Just repeating what I heard." *That's the truth, Rolle's words.*

He's ringing up the chips and looks at you, nodding. "Yeah, right. I got you. I got you. Guess my cousin's Camaro's ain't nothing."

"I wouldn't go that far," *you say, grabbing the Doritos.* "But it's no Porsche."

You look out and see the big Dodge is gone, no other cars. And the clerk here is clearly on your side. Looking good. You're vapor inside two minutes. You smile and say goodbye, pushing through the door, halfway to the car, things unwinding now and stopping you dead.

Straight ahead.

Twenty-five yards.

Cop car rolling this way.

Chapter Twenty

HOME SWEET HOME.

Las Palmas Apartments, number 1321, off 16th Street, hotter than a piece of sheet metal left in Hell's front yard. Once inside you strip down to your T-shirt and underwear on the way to the kitchen. You grab a can of Diet Coke, which you leave unopened and press against your forehead.

"Let's welcome you home, baby."

There's little you admire more than a man devoted in that arena. But now? You hope he'll let it go. You open the can, but the Diet Coke isn't cold enough. You suddenly empathize with Bobby B's endless quest for hot tea water; nothing worse than a beverage that's not quite the right temperature.

"C'mon, baby."

You open the refrigerator, search for a colder can, and walk back into the combination dining-living room, two cans of Diet Coke pressed on each side of your throbbing head. This is the weigh station to your new life: a retro diner table with two chairs that don't match, a green chaise that smells like cat piss (Rolle pulled the couch from the Las Palmas trash Dumpster), and a 52-inch

Sony that's one of the newer rear-projection models, which means it's roughly the size of a Volkswagen Beetle. Rolle took it in trade from a TV salesman for making the invoices disappear when the guy had his motor home painted and pinstriped. Rolle is on the chaise with his shirt off, smiling. Can't he give you, like, a few minutes to catch your breath? Take a shower? Unwind a little. You open one of the cans, shaking your head, and take a drink. He pats the couch with his hand.

"Come on baby. Missed you bad."

You don't know what to say. "I have to go. Somewhere."

"Go? We just got you home. You ain't even showed me the money, baby."

You pick up your purse, unzip, and start tossing stacks of tens and twenties at Rolle.

"The hell's this?"

"Your little Scottish buddy didn't make it to the bank." You stop throwing money when there's what looks like $10,000 left in the purse. Your end that you just earned.

"I'm just keeping mine this time."

"Say what?"

"My ten grand. I earned it, and I'm keeping it. There's five for you. And I'm not doing any more, so we might as well go to the banks now and split up the rest."

"Why you buggin'? We got us a deal. We almost all the way home."

"Yeah, well... the deal's been revised. I can't do this anymore."

"Or what?" The smile gone, sinking back onto the couch. "Why you playing? Ain't I been nothing but good to you?"

You step back toward the door, wishing now you could bolt, except you ditched your jeans, socks and shoes. You feel guilty again. He's right. He has been good. In a bad sort of way. Damn, he does look amazing with his shirt off. He stands up, walks over and presses up against you, backing you against the door. He puts his hands on either side of your head and leans in so close you can smell the weed on his breath. He kisses you. Slow. Romantic. Just the way you love to be kissed. A comforting rush of adrenaline washes through your body, and all of a sudden you feel safe again. Danger is safety. Safe is dangerous. Even with the AC blasting, your hands are sweaty. Rolle has you pinned against the door, your heart racing, mixture of fear and excitement. His eyes are red and half-closed now, but they're the kind of eyes you can't resist, the kind that make a girl revise plans.

"Baby's getting all funny on me. We're cool, baby. You just need to relax here."

"Rolle, no. I can't. No more."

"Baby now, come on. Why you trippin'? Who done hooked us up into this gig? Who been carrying you since the day you showed up here? Who's been doing all that? Huh? No pressure. No demands. We came up with this together, and that's the way we gonna finish it. See what I'm saying?"

"Please. Don't."

"You know I need all of my end and more to get opened up. I'm this close to my dream, baby."

"I can't do this again, I just can't."

"Sure you can, baby. Look, it's real simple: we put this $15,000 with the other money. Just like we always do. You're the star, baby. You're my star. You done it clean all those times already. Ain't nothing bad gonna happen now."

"Rolle..." you hesitate, wondering if you'll tell him. You need to tell him. You need to tell someone. The old life. The new life. Who you were and who you're going to be. All right, who you're *trying* to be.

"Something bad. I did something bad."

"Ah baby, remember what I said. Ain't no one need to shed a single tear over some insurance company. They the only ones now on all fours feeling the thump-thump. You thirsty?" He disappears into the kitchen and comes back holding two longneck beers. "Want one?"

Barter it.

Sell it.

Give it away.

The metal door is hot against your back, unopened cans still pressed against your forehead. "Did you hear what I said?"

"Said a lot of stuff, baby."

He offers the beer again, and you shake your head. He sets one bottle on the table, opens the other, and takes a long pull. Wipes his mouth.

You look inside yourself, wondering what's left.

Not now.

Not enough strength to say what you need to say.

"Tell me again?" he asks.

"Never mind."

Your stomach twists into knots again. You start to cry. Rolle tells you not to worry, he's got you, and hugs you while he rubs your back. The cold beer bottle makes you jump when it touches your arm. You drop both soda cans onto the carpet.

deep wicked freaky.

Three words that come to you in a dream after you cry yourself to sleep.

The night Singer dies.

The night you watch this kid ZigZag lose his only friend. You're hugging this lanky 15-year-old, neither of you saying a word while the nurses quietly work around you. Two people you barely know, and you cry yourself to sleep that night when you get back, the two vampires out prowling for easy money.

Something changes, except you don't know then what to call it.

Awareness.

Says how your life starts to unravel when Mom pulls her midnight move.

Says how you'll trade three weeks and ten times for $100,000 and get goose eggs from Rolle until you drop ten times.

Says how you'll head west to escape your life and end up within throwing distance of one-in-three Papa Jet, how you find out about him same week he's scheduled to die, same week you decide to start boosting cars.

Says how you can run, but you can never escape, not ever, from the three words that have become your life.

Rolle fiddling with the remote and then kissing you. Now pulling away and turning his head toward the 52-inch Sony every time the crowd noise gets louder.

Four months.

"Do we have to have the game on?"

"Eighth inning, baby. Two on, one out." Then, inexplicably, "You know who makes all the baseballs for the Major Leagues?"

"No, but the suspense is killing me."

"Rawlings. Know where they make 'em? About a million balls a year?"

"Rolle—"

"Costa Rica. Hand-sew every one. It's a beautiful game. It's the small details."

You half heartedly try to wave him off, but he leans in and kisses you again. The mood is gone, left out there somewhere on the black highway. You push him away. The crowd cheers, which pulls his attention back to the TV, and he stares at someone running the bases. You pick up the bong, stir the bowl with a match, and take a long hit that makes you cough.

The high creeps up the back of your skull and slows down the world, inserts blocks of space between everything. Too tired and numb to care. He turns his attention back to you, staring at you for a few seconds like he's looking for where he left off. Then an "Oh yeah" look, and he leans his head forward with his tongue leading the way. You turn your head away just before and stare at the baseball game.

THE next morning, alone, you're parked in *America's Ride* across the street from the nursing home.

Normal people visit their sick grandpa.

According to Mom's call, supposedly yours is in there.

One-in-three Papa Jet, pushing 80, no clue you exist.

Even after twelve-plus hours of sleep, you feel groggy and depleted. When you got up this morning, you were relieved to see Rolle passed out in front of the TV (still on). The collection of empty Budweiser bottles was considerably larger than when you left him there last night, crawled into bed and found instant oblivion.

You're glad that Rolle never joined you in the bed and even happier you slipped away in his van this morning without having to talk to him. A bagel and a large iced cappuccino to go, and here you sit wondering whether you're actually going to go in there.

As soon as you think about your dad and mom, the anger rises in your stomach and then crystallizes into a hard lump in your chest. Why should you do anything for either of them?

Silence. The same pain and despair.

Who needs any of it. You shake your head and take a sip.

One-in-three Papa Jet's nursing home is in a neighborhood a lot like the places Rolle drops you to pick up stolen cars: industrial, lots of chain-link fences, garbage and rusted metal, the irritating roofing tar you smell everywhere you go in Phoenix this time of year. There's a boombox somewhere nearby with distorted Spanish music blasting. The nursing home itself is a complex of one-level, white-brick buildings all past due on paint. Some of the windows are cracked, and the brown grass out front and between the buildings is more dirt than grass. There's two sagging, sad-looking palm trees on either side of the sign:

SILVERCREST
Assisted Living

You step from the lukewarm confines of the van into the searing heat that, according to the radio, is headed toward 109°F. The heat and the distorted music are giving you a headache. You close the door and catch a reflection of yourself in the window of the car parked next to the van. You sip your iced cappuccino and take a long, deep breath. Asking the watery blob: *You really want to do this?* The watery blob says nothing.

Inside Silvercrest.

You feel a lump rise in your throat from the hospital smell as you drop your empty cup into the trash can by the door, wondering again if you should just turn around and walk out before anyone sees you. There's a front desk, nobody around. You can hear an old woman screaming something about find the jump-rope or she's going back to Kentucky. You can't see anyone, but her shrieks echo up and down the stained white linoleum hallway. *Disinfectant.* You get a big whiff that makes your stomach turn.

Not you.

Not now.

Not ever.

"You all right?"

There's a guy standing there in blue hospital scrubs, a guy your size (short). For some reason you think of one of Jordan's dancer friends. She had a tattoo next to her pubic hair that was a horizontal, flattened hand and the words MUST BE THIS TALL TO RIDE.

"Some water or something?" he says.

You shake your head, pull it together. "I was, uh… I'm looking for—"

He smiles, opens a three-ring notebook on the desk and flips a couple pages. "You have a name?"

"Jenna. But I go by 'Jet.'"

He smiles. "I meant for who you're visiting."

You feel stupid. Give him a smile. "Right. Duh?"

"Actually, though, I think I know who you're here to see."

This catches you off-guard. He smiles and closes the notebook. "I've been here almost a year. You're his first visitor."

"I'm whose first visitor?"

"Papa Jet."

You don't say anything. *Do you really want to do this?*

"Am I right? Because you said 'Jet,' so I'm assuming, you know. Same last name."

Same last name.

Same last name as one-in-three Papa Jet. You smile. "You must think I'm, like—God, I swear I didn't even know he was here. Can you believe that? Long story, but my dad, well, if you can even call him—"

"Sorry, you can't do that in here."

"I can't bitch about my dad?"

He smiles and points, and then you realize he means the unlit Marlboro Light you're waving around. "Oh I'm sorry. Of course." You try to slide the cigarette back into the pack, except it breaks. Your hand is shaking.

"Hey, good news is that you're here. Right? Most of these people? Never get a single visitor. You'd think kids, grandkids, friends?" He shakes his head. "No one."

You look for a trash can, which he produces from under the desk.

"Thanks."

"He talks about you."

"Me? Really? I've never met him."

"Really?" He looks confused.

You shake your head. "Long story."

He thinks about this and nods slowly. "He's talked about how he took care of his granddaughter for a year when she was little. Was that you? Or a sister?"

"Could be. I mean, not a sister. There is no sister. So could be me. Maybe he's just confused. Aren't a lot of them like that, like super-confused?"

He nods.

"All I know is I don't remember ever meeting him." The disinfectant smell is really making your stomach turn. Why are you here again? "I should leave."

"You OK?" He moves over this way.

"Yeah." You're about to throw up. "You know where I can get a Coke or something?"

He's got a hand on your elbow, steadying you. "Sure. We've got a pop machine here, or there's a Circle K a few blocks up."

"Circle K." You pull away and start to walk out. Woozy.

"You sure you're OK?" he says. "Look, I'm going on break and need to go anyway. I could drive you up there. You're completely white."

You look back and nod, OK. He looks harmless. Works at a nursing home. Nice smile. "Great. I need to let my supervisor know; be right back."

Heading south on 16th Street. Your breathing is back to normal. Now you're trying to figure why you freaked out. You stop at a light, six cars back, middle lane, surrounded by other vehicles. Everyone's windows are up, air conditioners full speed. Then you see a big guy, in a droopy tank top, hunched over in a Honda Civic with all the windows down—no shirt, hairy man-boobs and shoulders, face soaked—poor dude's got no AC.

You adjust the vents to direct the flow into your chest, and the cool air on your wet shirt gives you a quick chill. You are impressed with this mystery guy's ride, that is, not the car itself—a '70s Buick-something that's got style but could use a visit to Meryl Mack's—but rather the cooling power, both temperature and air-flow velocity, of the AC. Like Rolle's van, this low, wide Buick is all about space. The traffic light changes, Buick rolls.

"Man, this air conditioner is awesome."

He signals and moves to the left lane. "What's your first name again?"

"Jenna. But I go by my last name now. You know, I had a brand new Mustang, but this ride's nice. You totally can't even feel the road." You dig in your purse. "Mind if I smoke?"

"No problem."

You pull out a cigarette, crack the window and light up. Deep drag. Yes, that's better.

"So you go by 'Jet'?"

You look over at him. "Long story."

He nods and smiles.

"Quick version…" You tip your head up to the opening and exhale smoke. "There is no such thing. But basically, my life as 'Jenna' was messed up, so I left her back east when I moved out here. This is my new life." You pause and exhale, scan the white-hot hell. "Well, sort of. It's almost my new life. Sounds mental, I know."

"Not at all."

You look over at him and shake your head. "Liar."

He's laughing. "You graduating or something?"

"Graduating?" Now there's a concept.

"Like what you said about your new life starting soon."

You take another long pull and look at him, thinking it's cool how he takes care of those old people—*your* old people—and drives this '70s Buick. Then you think he must be gay. That's cool. You stare at the smoke curling off the tip of the cigarette. Then you forget what he said and just let it go. The light changes and traffic starts creeping forward. He's smiling.

"Your grandpa."

"What about him?"

"You've really never met him?"

"Really never. Didn't even know he was alive until a few weeks ago."

"Really. How's that happen?"

"Story of my life." Same three words.

"How so?"

"Truthfully, I'd rather hear about him."

"Well, he's been there since I started. Almost a year now. You get to know the people there and try to guess what their kids or grandkids will be like, and wonder if they'll ever show. I never expected anyone to show up for him. Wish you could have seen him three months ago."

"What do you mean?"

He hesitates, runs his finger along a crack in the dashboard. "Before the stroke. He's not the same now. Comes and goes, but he's not the same."

Silence except for the hum of the AC.

"You know he had the stroke on his birthday, the day he turned 77?"

You didn't know that, but you nod anyway. You're not sure what to say.

"He'll be happy to see you."

You just nod. "So you never told me your name."

"Sorry. Nick."

"Nick what?"

"Nick Sands."

"Nick Sands. Cool name."

"Yeah?"

"Yeah. Simple. Direct. Just like, Nick Sands. Any questions? No? Good, deal the cards."

He nods his head and laughs. You take a long pull on your cigarette and flick the ashes out the opening. "I got a cartoon name."

"Cartoon?"

"Yeah, like Jessica Rabbit. Fred Flintstone. Mine's Jenna Jet. Sounds like a cartoon name."

"Maybe. It's not so bad."

Nick Sands, blue scrubs that look like he ironed them ten minutes ago. Just your everyday nice guy, one of those average kids from high school that are sort of invisible. Still 70/30 that he's gay. Just has that certain vibe.

"So anyway, Nick Sands, the smell where you work. You know?"

"You get used to it."

He wheels into the Circle K (in Phoenix, there's a Circle K every 30 yards) and, like a true Arizona shade-seeker, parallels the gas pumps covered by a large awning. He leaves the engine running to keep the Freon pumping. You hold your hand against the vent, coldest AC you've ever felt in your life, building or vehicle. Nick's car is a good place to be.

"What do you want to drink? My treat."

"Thanks. Large Diet Coke."

"Be right back." He gives you a smile and climbs out of the Buick.

You haven't really met anyone outside of Rolle's circle. It's nice to just chill, shoot the breeze. Sort of makes you feel normal. Sort of. You can see Nick in the store, standing at the drink dispensers. You pull open the ashtray and stub the smoke. Now he's walking back this way with two giant cups. He doesn't say anything, just hands you the Diet Coke. He climbs in and takes a long drink. The big Buick engine is rumbling.

You think about the double life.

The insanity that's not quite real except when you're out there. Ten hours each including airport time back to Phoenix. That's $100,000 to you in 100 hours.

For some weird reason you want to tell Nick Sands about your old life, just unload everything you've been carrying around. But that would be mental. You light another cigarette and blow out smoke. Take a drink of Diet Coke, cup sweating fat water droplets. There's a long silence. The cumulative sleep debt has fried your brain to the point that you can't remember what you were thinking five seconds ago. Mind screen goes completely blank. You sit in the silence and let the cool air wash across you. Your shirt's dry now. You stare at a preppy guy pumping gas into his evergreen BMW (Bobby B isn't interested in any 3-Series). It's hot enough out there to kill the living, so you're grateful to be sitting in a Buick the size of Lower Manhattan, AC vents pumping air directly from base camp on Everest. Your own private Himalayan pipeline of iced O_2.

"So, Jet, you ready to go back and see your grandpa?"

AC hum. *Grandpa.* You're not sure what to say. You're not sure what you feel. You're tired. Confused. Why are you making such a big deal out of this?

"I should just go see him. Right?"

He nods. "It's like this for a lot of people. We don't do so well with our elderly in this culture. It's because we're uncomfortable with our own mortality. At least that's my opinion."

You suck on the straw. "I've got this really good friend back east who talks about the same kind of stuff." You take another hit off the cigarette and stub it. You still need to call Dale and see how he's doing (if you can find his number).

Nick glances at his watch. "I should get back. You know, you shouldn't feel bad if you don't want to see him."

"Really?

He's shaking his head. "Not at all. And I would make sure he knew you came."

"Thanks. That's sweet."

He slips the car into Drive and wheels back into the sunlight. Then you ask, "Would you go in there with me?"

"To his room?"

You nod.

He nods back at you. "Sure."

You light another cigarette.

One-in-three Papa Jet.

Papa Jet gets a stroke for his birthday.

Papa Jet sees his granddaughter for the first time in 20-odd years.

You pull nicotine and watch storefronts blink in the scorching white light. So it's time. *Really?* Really.

You take a deep breath.

Prologue to your new life.

Time to go meet your one-in-three Papa Jet.

Chapter Twenty-One

STANDSTILL IN INDIO, CLOCK RUNNING. Rule #2 about to snag Jet times one. Number ten, redline, cracks spreading and tearing everything apart.

Bought it.

Sold it.

Gave it away.

Smooth and silent, cop car pulls up and angles in five feet from where you're standing, a single empty space between his car and the Porsche. You continue forward as the cop climbs out of his car. He's local police, not CHP, thank God.

"Morning," he says, smiling.

"Morning," you say without looking, opening the door. You don't look back, praying that he's on his way into the store. Except then he says, "Nice. Pretty fast, huh?" Guys and this car, here you go again. You turn around. He's a young guy, skinny, late 20s, moustache, dark sunglasses, decent shape. You smile and say, "Goes 70, I know that."

The cop laughs. He's sipping from a white foam cup. Steam trails. "Uncle had a car like that, lives out there in LA. You believe that? Could never live in LA. The people. Traffic. All those homeless. They got that AIDs out there. You heard about Magic Johnson, right? He got the AIDs out there. Hell no I wouldn't live there. You?"

You shift on your heels, smiling. "I like the beach."

"Yeah, beach is nice. Except for all the people again. Wonder if you can get the AIDs from the ocean, you think? Probably. Won't catch this old boy in that cesspool ocean. Anyway, my uncle's was kind of a dark green, like a, you know, what do you call it?" He looks to the clear blue sky for the answer.

"Turquoise?" the goatee kid offers. You turn and see him. Great, he's joined the party and is squatting by the ice machine smoking a cigarette.

The cop turns and says, "No, Kim, not turquoise. You ever seen a car turquoise? A ring maybe you bought off the reservation, but no car you seen is called 'turquoise.'"

Goatee Kim considers this before saying, "Maybe I seen one."

"No, you haven't." Goatee Kim looks disappointed. The cop says, "This was green except more darker. You know?"

This is the kind of minutiae guys like to climb down inside and stay in for hours, wandering around among the meaningless trivia. Especially Barney Fife here and goatee Kim, who takes a deep drag and coughs and says, "What, like metallic?"

The cop shakes his head. "Is metallic a color? Metallic isn't a color all on its own."

"Can be," goatee Kim says. "What about lime metallic?"

"Lime metallic? As in lime metallic. You just proved my point."

Goatee Kim laughs. "Shut up."

The cop sighs like a frustrated father. "Anyway, not lime. I said more darker lime's even brighter than turquoise. And besides, it wasn't even metallic neither. Just straight."

"You mean like forest?" goatee Kim says.

There's a pause before the cop says, "OK, yeah, like that except what do you call that?" He's snapping his fingers.

"Trees?" goatee Kim says.

Barney Fife shoots a look that takes another chunk out of the kid's self-esteem. "Trees?" The cop just shakes his head and then laughs. "Yep, just got me that new Porsche, Kim, and it's 'trees metallic.' You are dumber than a neon box of nothing."

"Shut up," goatee Kim says. "You could—"

"Evergreen!" the cop yells, clapping once. "Evergreen. Shit, isn't that something when it's stuck right at that gate between your brain and your tongue like a hair you can't spit? Evergreen."

"Evergreen," goatee Kim says. "Lime's better."

"Maybe if you're making margaritas. What color you call that there?" the cop asks. "I mean, obviously it's yellow, but you got the official name?"

"Speed Yellow."

"Speed Yellow," Barney Fife repeats. "See what I tell you, Kim? Speed Yellow." Now sipping his coffee and moving this way.

No, don't come over here.

Go away.

Question is, curious or suspicious about the car? Or both?

"What year?" he asks.

"Brand-new."

"No shit? Wow, surely set you back a few stacks, huh?"

"Just a few. My fiancé's, actually."

"Lucky guy," he says, smiling. He may have just answered your question.

"Well, I really should get going. Meeting a friend for breakfast when I get there."

"Sure would love to have me one of these someday. You mind me asking, you know, ballpark, what one of these sets you back?"

Yes, you mind. None of your business. "Low six figures."

He whistles. "No shit? Low six? You hear that, Kim? Low six you want one of these. Kim there will be on two wheels, as in bicycle, pretty much for the duration."

"Shut up, will not. I even seen a Ferrari come through few months back, quarter-mil."

The cop whistles again. "Low six, quarter-mil, don't make any difference. Too rich for this farmer's blood. Guess I don't stand a chance getting a date with a girl like you, huh?"

"You couldn't get a date with her you had a private plane."

"Shut up, Kim. Could too."

You smile. Exactly what part of 'fiancé' did he not understand? "Well, nice talking with you."

"Hey, you too. You ever get tired of that fiancé, you know where to look me up." Then he gives you one of those cheesy little index finger salutes and a goofy smile.

Not in this lifetime or the next, pal. You glance back to see goatee Kim, who's shaking his head.

"You're such a dumb-ass," Kim says to the cop.

"Kim, shut your pimpled face before I shut it for you," the cop says, looking back.

While they're sparring you slide down into the cockpit, pull the door closed, and start the engine. The cop looks this way and smiles when he hears the engine, double thumbs-up. You smile back and pull away and watch just to make sure he's not going for his radio. You say aloud, "Just go in the store like the good boy you are."

Before turning onto the road you came in on, you watch in the rearview until he disappears into the store, where you suspect he and the clerk will compare notes on the hot babe in the Turbo Porsche, highlight of the year in Indio.

Finally, rolling back toward I-10. Holy shit, but do close calls get any closer than that?

Nothing but Indio in slumberland.

You check the rearview just to make sure.

Freedom.

You feel like you have the flu, stomach twisted and neck stiff, and you don't know if you can physically take this anymore.

Too much pressure.

Too much caffeine.

Too much risk.

You get back to I-10 and merge, winding through the gears with your thumb. There's a small truck that doesn't want to move to the left lane, so you grab one gear lower with your thumb and rocket past the truck on the right shoulder, then giggle in amazement when you look in the rearview and see how far ahead of him you already are. Racing past slow-moving Toyotas briefly blocks out the terror hanging around you. Then the familiar nightmare settles back in, a heavy blanket of sick fear you can't shake.

Two more hours.

Two more hours, and you're free.

You think about palm trees and ocean air, and breathe easier. You think about Mom, get out while the getting's good. And then you think about what Papa Jet said, letting it roll around for the first time. Maybe you at least check things out with Dad and give him a chance to tell you his side.

Chapter Twenty-Two

FIRST TIME YOU SEE ONE-IN-THREE PAPA JET, he's wearing a red cowboy hat and sunglasses and holding a jambox in his lap that looks like it could crush him. He's moving his head, off-beat, to a country song you've never heard because you've never heard any country song.

You turn and look back at Nick, who grins and shrugs his shoulders. You're standing in the doorway of the room with a Polaroid of Papa Jet pinned to the cork board on the door. The room is hot, small and stuffy, with a curtain hanging between the two beds. There's only one window, next to Papa Jet's bed, with the tattered blinds open just enough that you see the vibrant red bougainvillea leaves outside. The other bed is stripped down to a bare mattress.

One-in-three Papa Jet seems a lot better than you expected. Definitely not like someone who's supposed to die any day. He's not hooked up to any machines or IVs. In fact, there's no medical equipment in the room.

His body is small and wiry, yet looks hard and strong. You're guessing that's a cigarette that he rolled himself tucked behind his left ear, but it looks just like a joint. He either hasn't noticed you yet, or has and isn't acknowledging you. You turn back to Nick and whisper, "Should I wait until the song's over?"

"*Rhinestone Cowboy*," Nick says, laughing. "We still don't know where he got the tape, *Glen Campbell 20 Greatest Hits*, only one he has, so we all get to hear it over and over and over. At first you hate it and then, kind of grows on you."

Papa Jet.

Curled up on a gurney waiting to die?

Without stepping past the curtain, without exchanging a single word, without him even acknowledging your existence, you get this quick rush of hope that he's your grandfather. You feel Nick touch the back of your arm.

"Go ahead," like a parent nudging a scared child toward a goat at the petting zoo. You hesitate, take a deep breath and walk toward the bed. Then Papa Jet sees you, turning his head this way and leaning back to peek under the sunglasses. He's watching you move toward the bed. Then Nick comes up from behind, slipping past you and hitting the STOP button.

"Papa Jet, you've got a visitor."

Papa Jet doesn't say anything, just stares at you except you can't see his eyes through the glasses. Then he reaches and pushes the PLAY button, and Glen Campbell picks up again.

"Papa Jet," Nick says, hitting STOP again and wrestling the jambox away, "you have a very special visitor today." Nick sets the blaster on the white linoleum.

Now you feel weird. Stupid. What an idiot you are for showing up here. The room feels like it's closing in, getting hotter and hotter, and all you want to do is blast out and never come back. No one says anything.

You stare at Papa Jet.

Nick drops the silver rail on the bed and stands with one hand on Papa Jet's shoulder. Papa Jet is looking straight ahead and scratching the thin stubble of white across his chin. Then he adjusts his red cowboy hat, tipping it up slightly, and pulls off the sunglasses. He looks at you for the first time, deep blue eyes and a determined gaze that really pops against his face.

"Aren't you going to say hello?" Nick says to Papa Jet.

One-in-three Papa Jet's shoulders rise and fall noticeably with each breath, a raspy sound pushing out each exhale. The disinfectant smell is still lodged in your sinuses. Then he lifts his left hand, curling his fingers back and forth as though he's reaching out for you. You walk forward until you touch hands, now clasping his bony hand and holding it tightly. Nick steps aside and starts out the room. He gives you a wink before leaving.

One-in-three Papa Jet coughs quietly for what seems like forever. You hold his hand, not sure what to say or do. You can feel the sweat trickling down the middle of your back, his hand getting wet between your palms. Then he leans back and settles into the pillow, the cowboy hat tipping forward and falling off his head. You pick up the hat and set it next to him. His thin hair is matted to his head from the hat.

"That hat's the bomb," you say, smiling, then realizing. "I like your hat." He signals with his other hand for you to come closer.

Closer.

You lean in.

Closer, until your ear is inches from his mouth.

First thing one-in-three Papa Jet ever says to you comes out slow: "Treat you goddam children. Here. You. Can't let. Me. Flip my lid. Here." He squeezes your hands harder when he says this. You don't know what to say. "Get me out. Beautiful you." He coughs. Now you see what Nick meant about the stroke. You strain to follow what he's saying.

"Worth. While you."

Papa Jet curled up on a gurney waiting to die.

Talk about uncomfortable. You don't know what to say.

"Please. You," he says, his eyes catching you off guard and making you feel sad and sick and scared and helpless. How dare your parents pawn this off on you. "Goddam prison. Here. The food. Horrible! Please."

Do you tell him, surprise, there's a one-in-three chance that you're his granddaughter? Ask him what he's been up to for his entire life? He takes a few deep breaths and stares into your eyes. You tuck the sheet up around his V-neck T-shirt. He lifts his head off the pillow and says, "Take me..." His voice trails off into nothing as he runs out of breath. You lean closer, but he doesn't say anything. This is not the conversation you envisioned with your newly discovered grandfather. You had this image of a rocking chair and the little-girl you in her grandpa's lap while he tells stories that make you laugh. Even being here feels weird. He shakes his head, frustrated. You endure another extended silence and then breathe out and smile. You try to laugh away the tension and squeeze his hand.

One-in-three grandfather in a red cowboy hat with his own personal country soundtrack. Dream that's become your life. Now he's smiling and nodding. Odds are against you that he's blood. He closes his eyes and his mouth goes slack, relief spreading across his wrinkled face. He takes a few deep breaths and nods with his eyes still closed. You reach up and move the cowboy hat to the little dresser next to the bed, then sit in the chair and take his hand. His breathing is getting heavier, eyes still closed. You don't plan to say this, it just comes out: "Grandpa?"

He lifts his eyelids halfway and stares at you with this distant gaze. Is he looking back into his mind's eye to something he sees in you? Or does he even really know what's happening? He's looking at you, but you can't tell if he's truly here or not. Then he closes his eyes again without saying anything.

"You rest. I'll come back later."

You think about your first conversation with Papa Jet because it's better than thinking about the money you don't get unless you run all ten. When you step back into the hallway, you see Nick with his arm around a white-haired lady in a blue sweater, walking this way. She's looking down, neither of her feet coming off the floor when she walks. Nick sees you and smiles and says, "There's a waiting room out front. I'll be right there."

Before today, you've never been to a nursing home. After you get used to the stinging disinfectant smell, the next thing you notice is that, besides Papa Jet and Nick Sands, there are few other men. *Silvercrest* is standing-room-only with widows. Women slumped in wheelchairs in the hallway, asleep, like stalled cars abandoned along the highway in a snowstorm.

Women screaming about jump-ropes and going back to Kentucky.

Women propped up in hospital beds watching TV at supersonic decibel levels.

Alone.

Waiting.

Just waiting for the inevitable.

You tip your head back against the brick wall and close your eyes. Everything you've been pushing away comes flooding back as soon as you let your guard down. Like how your life is still locked in that narrow groove at 140 miles an hour. Twenty-five-foot concrete walls on either side.

Stop, you get destroyed.

Slow down, you get destroyed.

The only way out is straight ahead.

Push the accelerator through the floor and let the road vibration carry you to the other side. Just disconnect and go numb. Block out the terror of the bleak desert night. Ride the disconnect to your freedom.

"How's he doing?" Nick asks.

You snap back. "What?"

"He asleep?" Nick asks.

You nod. "I think." Nick glances at his wrist.

"This is the best time to see him. First few hours of the day, he's closer to his old self. Almost. Then he gradually gets worse throughout the day, especially his speech. Gets tired. Energy goes way down." After a long pause, Nick asks, "He say anything about you busting him out of here?"

"Sort of, yeah."

Nick re-ties the drawstrings on his scrub pants. "Yeah, ever since he came here, every day, he talks about how much he wants to get out. Breaks your heart. One woman we had insisted we take her to Washington D.C. because she left her diamond earrings at the White House. One guy said he was Audrey Hepburn's lover, and if we didn't call her and tell her where he was, she was going to die of a broken heart. Strange coincidence, but we'd just watched *Roman Holiday* the week before."

"How do you work here?"

"You could take him."

"Me?" Do you tell him about the 33.3 percent chance?

"Yeah, just getting him out of here for a few hours would mean the world to him. Hasn't been out of here since I started. Almost a year. That's a long time to be cooped up in this place. We wheel them outside when we can, but that's about it."

"That's disgusting, is what it is." Grandfather or not, you consider what Nick just said. "Tell you what. I'll be back. Tomorrow morning. We'll see how it goes."

"That would make his week. His *year*." He walks over and smiles. "I just want you to know it's really great you came to see him. He knows even if it doesn't seem like it."

You nod. "I guess so." You smile. You can just tell this Nick Sands is one of the good ones, and you're glad he's been around for Papa Jet. Awareness. You smile at him again and dig in your purse for your cigarettes.

LAS Palmas 1321, AC cranked down to 72 (Rolle doesn't like it when you do this because of the electric bill, so once you ice down the place, you'll sneak the dial back to 80). Thankfully, no Rolle when you get back here, although he does leave a note:

> *Baby, please don't disappear in my van when I got multiple tasks.*
> *Back at you soon. Big love, Rolle*

Who knows where he went, but with no car, unless he called one of his friends, it wasn't far, which means you don't have much time to yourself.

Time to crack the *Double-Blind, Two-Box Lock-Up.* Maybe find a statement or receipt or some little scrap of paper that will lead you to that bank, because you hold the key to get the money key. You wouldn't steal it, just take your cut, leave his and be done.

Start your new life.

You've already been through the obvious places: dresser drawers (9mm Browning automatic pistol, a box of bullets, a *Hustler* magazine), closet (more old *Hustler* magazines), shoe boxes, between the box spring and mattress (a purple pot pipe Rolle accused you of losing first week you were here), freezer (film canisters full of weed) and kitchen cupboards.

You know you've hit bottom when you're sitting in the bedroom closet checking inside his shoes. The little slip of paper that will lead you to your cut does not exist.

You. Can't let. Me. Flip my lid. Here.

You try to push the words away, but they linger like the sting of that disinfectant smell. Papa Jet. Meanwhile, you're on hands and knees in the bedroom closet looking for God-knows-what. As Dale always says, everywhere you go, there you are. You slump back against the wall, burying yourself in the cool, muted confines of the hanging clothes. Rolle is too smart to leave clues to his bank. You have no interest in hurting him, you just want what's yours. Then you hear the front door open.

"Jet! You here?"

Great.

"Jet!" the voice moving this way down the hall and then, "What the?" From the sound of his voice, he's in the hallway by the thermostat. You hear the AC switch off. You crawl out from the closet and slide onto the bed just as Rolle walks in the bedroom. He gives you a weird look, scratching his cheek, then a wide grin spreading across his face, pointing at you, "Now that's what I'm talking about, baby," walking this way, sunglasses on his head, unzipping his shorts.

"Time for some face time."

Then you're kissing, but you're somewhere else, thinking about that Nick Sands, how you're glad he's been there since Papa Jet went in.

"You OK, baby?" Rolle asks, pulling away.

"Yeah. Fine."

"You a million miles away, baby."

"Just a little tired."

Rolle shakes his head and drifts away. You're thinking about how hard it's going to be to leave here when the time comes. And as much as you try to push it away, that time is now. Last car or not, money or not, the little alarm has gone off. Awareness. Except Papa Jet clouding the escape plan.

"You hear me, baby?" Rolle asks, sticking his face out of the bathroom, his mouth foamed with toothpaste.

You have no idea what he just said but you nod anyway, and he goes back to brushing his teeth. If only you could find that money key. You pull in a deep breath and flop back onto the pillow, your shoulders tense as you play with the idea in your mind.

CHAPTER TWENTY-TWO

"You going out tonight?" you ask, praying he'll say yes.

"No."

"Why not? What about Victor and the guys?"

He steps from the bathroom back into the bedroom, naked, and just stands there. He's totally gorgeous. He's all muscles and flat stomach and smooth, dark skin. Then he wiggles it at you and says something stupid. What is it with guys, how they have to do that? Then he says, "Victor and Scott probably be coming by later. Crew be chilling here tonight."

Definitely not the answer you want to hear.

Chapter Twenty-Three

DEEP WICKED FREAKY.

    Says how you go nine times no snags and end up here on number ten: 5:58 a.m., *California wasteland, grooving through black desert in a stolen Porsche 911 Turbo, Polk* *Audio after-markets pumping new Pantera, palms wet on leather, burning a Marlboro,* *pressed block of crisp C-notes on the back end when Bobby B takes title in a few hours if—* *and it's the Queen Mother Bitch of all ifs—the headlights in the rearview aren't wired to* *CHiPs, Jon and Ponch pals looking to take you down.*

    Headlights full-frame.

    BOOM, red and blue bursts against black morning sky.

    Slow.

    Gravel.

    Idle.

    You think about firepower.

    Cop door slamming back there.

Footsteps and a flashlight beam. Standard police procedure, he says. Short stare and shake your head before turning and laying hands on glossy Speed Yellow rooftop. Second time he's over the line. Sick. Throat parched back to silence.

Leather creaking, keys jingling.

Crappy cologne.

Lump rising in your throat.

Meat hooks finally leave your body.

Boots scraping gravel on pavement.

Acid bubbling up in your throat. We done? Just about. Let's step into my office.

Back seat of the cruiser, hands cuffed in front, police radio that sounds legit even though you still wonder, "cop" writing on a clipboard. What you're telling yourself is this will all be over soon.

Tell yourself the smell of sweat and drugstore cologne and the vinyl seat will not make you puke if you just don't think about it. Saying how this doesn't matter because you can't feel anything, reminding you that your entire body is numb. Telling you not to worry, you'll walk.

You start thinking about options if he wants to take you back to the box. Would you help yourself by giving up Bobby B? You're not sure. Rolle's name, though, would never have to come up.

Filling out a job application:

Q: Have you ever been convicted of a felony?

A: Well, no, not really, unless you, well, OK, here's the thing . . . there was the one grand theft auto, ten counts actually, but I can explain . . .

"Car comes back clean," he says through the glass. "No warrants on you." He's tapping the dashboard with his Bic, staring off toward the purple horizon, sun breaking behind you. "But I'll tell you what, I got me some probable cause here, all kinds of it. Something ain't right with you being out here with that car this time of day."

He doesn't look at you in the rearview, talking to his clipboard. "So you know what that means." It's not a question.

You do, but you say nothing.

He climbs out, slams his door, and leans toward the passenger window, tapping it with his Bic. "You sit tight while I go tear that car apart and see what you might be hiding."

Chapter Twenty-Four

DEEP WICKED FREAKY.

The same dream over and over like some weird message from the universe, rolling east now on McDowell in *America's Ride*, AC cranked and still sweating, lazy groove thumping from a stereo that definitely wasn't installed when this bucket rolled off the line in Detroit, that familiar sick feeling in your stomach as you drive back to your past.

Back inside Silvercrest.

One-in-three Papa Jet out cold. You're sitting next to his bed, Nick dropping the rail for you when you get back. You're holding Papa Jet's left hand between both your hands. Silvercrest is quieter now, no screaming women. All you can hear is a game show on a TV down the hall. Nick says most of the residents, at least the ones who can get out of bed, are on the other side of the building eating dinner. You want to wake Papa Jet and ask him the question straight out.

Seventy-seven.

Papa Jet curled up on a gurney waiting to die.

You hear someone walk in, then Nick stepping around the ugly green curtain drawn down the center of the room. You don't turn your head, in the hope that Nick will take the hint and slip away without saying anything.

Alone time with Papa Jet.

A few seconds pass and, thankfully, Nick is quietly gone. You pull your hand away and pick up the boombox, press PLAY. Papa Jet's only tape, Glen Campbell, nothing you'd ever buy. The song starts with this soothing melody on a guitar (banjo?). Unlike heavy metal, you can understand Gentle on My Mind without having to read lyrics. Some dumb country song, but it's not horrible. You listen to the song and stare at Papa Jet's forehead while it plays. When the song ends, you rewind and play it again, this time picking up more of the lyrics. When the song finishes again, you glance around the room to make sure no one's watching, and play the song a third time. You'll never admit that you like this Glen Campbell guy, whoever he is.

Seventy-seven years. A one-in-three granddaughter out there somewhere. Gentle on his mind. You feel like a complete geek already, but the song makes you tear up. OK. You're mental. When the song ends, you hit STOP and pull a tissue from the box on the nightstand.

Whatever. Get a grip, Jet.

You blow your nose, lean forward and kiss Papa Jet on the forehead. His skin is soft, smoothed out. His mouth has dropped open, and he's snoring lightly each time he inhales. Peaceful. Tension dissolved away. You don't know where this comes from, but it's out your mouth before you realize what you're saying: "Love you, grandpa."

LAS Palmas. Getting ready to be anywhere but here when Rolle's crew shows.

"Where you going?" Rolle asks.

"Out." You're standing in front of your underwear drawer with one towel tied around your head and another wrapped around your body.

"Out where?" Rolle is sucking on his favorite pipe, one you bought him on one of those perfect first afternoons when you'd just started your new life. He offers the burning pipe; you pass. "What up, baby? You trippin' again."

"I'm not—I just don't feel like talking right now." You make your selection from the drawer: tonight's all about the tent-sized granny panties and total cotton comfort.

"Sure looks like you trippin' to me."

"Rolle, come on. Not now, OK?" You grab your oldest and softest pair and a bra and head to the bathroom. You stop in the bathroom doorway and turn, Rolle right behind you. "Look. I'm sorry. I just need some space tonight."

"Yeah? Well you been all about the space, baby, distant as a star. You planning on rolling out of here soon? I been knowin' from the start we was temporary."

"I'm... you know. We don't ever really talk. Maybe, yeah. But not tonight or anything." You feel guilty when you say it.

He puts the lighter flame to the pipe and shrugs his shoulders as he pulls in a long hit. You don't know what else to say, so you close the bathroom door. He's talking through the closed door, mellowed out from the weed. Most people get stoned and just want to chill; Rolle talks even more than usual. Grand plans and schemes like you driving ten hot cars across the desert.

You smooth on face cream. You've got a lot of the $20-a-bottle stuff because Jordan had a friend who worked at a salon and got you the five-finger discount. You pause with your face inches from the mirror and squeeze a blackhead, but nothing comes out. You scan your forehead for a few seconds and then roll on deodorant. You drop the body towel and stare at yourself in the mirror.

You hate yourself naked.

You can barely stomach what you see. Speaking of stomachs, yours looks like triplets any day now. Make that quintuplets. You pump the lotion dispenser and start the all-over moisturizing.

"Baby, maybe I'll come in there right now and we could, you know. Just chill out. Know what I mean?"

Las Palmas was built way before you were born, all your stuff spread out on cracked green Formica. You look at yourself again in the mirror, the horror of your nakedness.

Gross.

Talk about a cow. You hate the shape of your breasts and the way the one droops down like that. You push it up, let it down, push it up, let it down. Disgusting.

You pull the towel off your head, bend over and towel-dry your hair before rubbing in gel. You look at the same brunette head you've had your whole life and wonder if you could go bright red like a punker. Or maybe platinum blonde? A change would be good. Maybe when you officially start your new life.

"Hold on, baby," Rolle says through the door. "Need to fix my bowl."

Next is your dual base powder. Jordan turned you on to the two-in-one, foundation-and-powder concept. You start applying with the little pad and smile, Jordan telling you, "Forget that liquid clay shit. You got to simplify, girl." You've given up on the freckles that don't ever smooth out no matter how much makeup you wear. And the eyebrows, didn't you just pluck two days ago? Two quick pinches with the eyelash curler, and now you're brushing on eye shadow. You like the clear-blue sparkle. Then you stretch your eyelid and paint a black line with a grocery-store special liner, two for a buck.

Rolle comes back to the door and starts going on about something. You tune him out while you uncap your $12 mascara and stare at the little brush. How long have you had this mascara? Maybe you should toss it? You go light, just a little to thicken your eyelashes and a quick pass to darken your eyebrows. Rolle is asking you something.

"What?" you ask, feeling the anger. Why did you ever listen to him in the first place?

"Damn, baby," he says. "Chill."

You lean in and use the lip liner and some boysenberry lipstick for a full, red look. Then you step back from the mirror and spritz all over with a body spray.

Back to the boobs; you are really hating on your boobs. How the right one hangs down lower and the way the left nipple looks all weird. The right one's a little bigger, too. You push up your right one with your hand, let it droop back down. And again, up and then down. Great, by the time you're 30, you'll be tucking that sucker into your belt. The other one isn't far behind. You hate the idea of cosmetic surgery, and the last thing you need is more size, but you'd give anything to be symmetrical and more perky, say, a full B. These things are too big and out of control.

As long as you're already disgusted, might as well go all the way. You dig under the sink and pull out the scale for the first time in three weeks. You'll be lucky if you don't pop the springs. You step on and lean to one side and pinch with one hand.

Sick.

You turn sideways, suck in your stomach, and run your hand up and down. What used to be flat has been replaced by a belly. You pinch and pull and squeeze both sides of your waist.

OK, totally disgusted. Not a huge roll, but definitely the start of one. You can't bear to look at the dial on the scale. Still naked and after a little prayer, you peek down at the dial.

128.

Holy crap. You've never been 128 in your life. 128? You yell again, "Is this scale right? Rolle?!"

A few seconds later, through the closed door, you hear, "What you yelling about?"

"Is this scale right?"

"Scale? Like a Swiss train."

"Never mind." You step off and push the evil thing behind the toilet with your foot.

"Then again," he says, giggling, "No wait; I was wrong. That's the one you need to add five pounds to whatever it says."

"Very funny." That's it. No solid food for the next six weeks. Carrot juice and water until you're back to 105. OK, 105 would be, like, 8th grade. That's a stretch. 115. Even 120. And Rolle can forget about seeing these jelly rolls ever again. You pick up the lotion again and rub the mountains of whale flab.

"So anyway I got us the hookup, Sunday night, two a.m. That's really Monday morning, I guess. You ready to go for the team one last time?"

You scrunch and shake your hair. Then, while you're safety-pinning a black piece of velvet around your neck, another bizarre idea pops into your head: Why not blow town in number ten and never come back? Bobby B hands you the shrink-wrapped cash on the back end, you walk off into the California sunset with $15,000 cash to start your new life. Leave the rest on ice.

Right. Just shut up, because you know you'd never do that to Rolle. Not to mention that fifteen grand won't last long in California, and what about Papa Jet? Shit. When did starting a new life get so complicated? What happened to the clean break? Go west, young woman. Except there you are right next to the family you're trying to escape. Awareness.

"Hey? You in there?" he asks.

"Yeah."

"So?" he asks.

"I'm sorry. What?"

"Baby, you ready to drive, right?"

"Sure. Whatever."

He's holding in a hit when he says, "Damn, baby, you don't sound so sure."

Still moisturizing. Your calves are like a couple of water balloons, squishy and totally disgusting, but not as squishy and disgusting as the cellulite that bubbles up on your thighs when you press in the lotion. You press your hand into your thighs and watch in disgust as the little pock marks ripple across your skin. You do it repeatedly: *Press, ripple, release. Press, ripple, release. Press, ripple, release.* You could practically vomit right now.

That's it. You're sticking to the diet this time no matter what. Starting tomorrow. Could someone please tell you at what point in the last year you became such a fat cow? You squeeze your giant marshmallow body into the bra and panties and suck in your stomach, which doesn't do anything to hide the little roll over the waistband. You pull your panties all the way up to your belly button to hide your disgusting muffin top. You rinse your hands and step back for a look. Well, could be better, could be worse. Story of your life. Rolle is still outside the door talking away. "… Bobby B said he needs all the turbo nine one ones he can get."

The way he says it makes you smile, reminds you of the way that kid ZigZag used to say numbers: nine one one.

"… anyway, I go, what the fuck difference does it make? And he's all, what? And I go, shit, dude, all pays the same."

All pays the same.

Bought it.

Sold it.

Gave it away.

If Rolle was your new life, you'd be able to tell him anything. Everything. But you can't. "So they already got one lined up?"

"Oh yeah, they all over that shit. Some rich bastard oncologist—that like an eye doctor?"

You let it go. No energy, he's stoned, what's the point? He continues, "Anyway, lives up in Scottsdale. They all ready to blow that up Sunday night, meet us at the drop spot after. Or is 'oncologist' the dude goes Dr. Jellyfinger on you?"

"Rolle... do I really want to hear this?"

Well, other than maybe dropping 20 pounds so you don't look like a sumo wrestler, you're ready. You open the door, slip by him and walk into the bedroom to the closet.

"Damn, baby, smell good."

He follows close, too close, sucking on that pipe like he's not already gone enough. You want to wear baggy jeans and a black, long-sleeved maternity shirt to hide the flab rolls. But this is September in Phoenix, 100-plus at midnight.

You grab your favorite Guess shorts and a black Lycra top that fits tight enough you can lose the bra. As you squeeze into your shorts, you wonder again exactly how you're supposed to have an anorexic body fat percentage *and* boobs that defy gravity?

Surgery, fasting and/or one-in-a-million genes.

Only problem, the genes God gave you all go, "Moo."

"My body's disgusting," you yell, throwing the hanger in your hand across the room. "I hate myself."

Rolle looks at you and, completely perplexed, offers the pipe. "Baby, you could be in *Playboy* with that body. You are so beautiful. You just bloated from your period."

You look at him and start to tell him.

He says, "Anyway, I think that's right."

You zip up and run a black belt through the loops. "What's right?"

CHAPTER TWENTY-FOUR

"'Gynecologist' we know is the pussy doctor."

You just look at him and shake your head. "Will you stop with that?"

"What?"

"That word. All the time with that word."

"Baby, you know brothers be calling me Dr. Pussy."

He's like a child. Like all men: little children.

"Call me that because I know so much about it. I got my Ph.D. at the Vagi-Nation University." He giggles.

It doesn't make sense, but what does it matter?

Now he's nodding. "OK, I think I got this. So 'oncologist' has to be the one doing the back-door booty calls. Dude's all 'Bend over and say 'ahhh.'"

Rolle sits on the edge of the bed and laughs, the burning pipe about to fall out of his hand. All he has on is a pair of black shorts. Dark-skinned beauty with a marble-carved body by Michelangelo. It's not fair that he looks that good without trying.

You pull on your shirt, then slip back to the bathroom for a final look and all-over spritz of perfume that came in this cute little portable bottle. You grab your purse and pull open the front door, Rolle still babbling from the bedroom, "What time you coming home, baby?"

"Proctologist," you yell back to the bedroom.

"What?"

Then before closing the door, you yell, "Proctologist. That's the one who sticks his finger up your butt."

Part III

River Card

Chapter Twenty-Five

YOU WATCH THE COP WORK THE CAR, glove box, passenger seat, driver's side. Then nose buried in the trunk. Then he slams the trunk and works a tooth with his tongue.

Goose eggs on search.

Radio spitting cop talk.

Handcuffs cutting wrists.

You watch him walk back this way and open the left passenger door. "Out."

You wiggle your butt off the seat and climb out of the cruiser. He sighs, giving you his creepy stare. "I'd say the best thing you can do is don't ever get in my crosshairs again." Nodding, looking back toward the sunrise.

"I can go then?"

He doesn't look at you, doesn't say a word.

You take a couple slow steps back toward the Porsche. Shit, your hands are still cuffed. Deep breath. You shuffle back toward him, like you're trying not to spook a wild dog, hold up your hands. "Sorry, can you . . ."

He slams the passenger door of his cruiser. Stares at you for a few seconds with that familiar dumb look on his face. "Clock's ticking, young lady."

You're not sure what he means, but it's definitely creepy. He says it again: "Clock is definitely ticking."

It's like he's trying to use Jedi mind tricks on you, make you say or do something you'll regret. You know better than to reach for the bait.

Then keys jangling.

When the cuffs fall away, you hesitate, fear burning a hole in your stomach. Then his hand squeezing your arm. "Back over here."

Pushing around on the other side of the Porsche. What the hell is this? Again? You turn to say something but he cuts you off with, "Eyes front and center, missy." Back over by the Porsche, staring across the glossy roof to the highway.

"Get those hands up," he says.

Hands on Speed Yellow.

"What you need, missy, is to learn how to respect the law. And out here, I'm the law. And if I'm the law, we both know what that makes you. You ready to go to school?" Then a weird laugh.

The bad dream just got worse.

Seconds, minutes. Silence. You're afraid to turn around. As you start to move your head you hear a door slam, gravel spit, cop car kicking a cloud of dust as he flips a hard "U" and burns rubber the other way. Huh? You just stare as the dust floats away. Numb. Wondering if this is part of the head games. Cat and mouse. Or if it's over.

You walk back to the car wiping away a tear.

You slide back down into the Porsche.

Slam the door.

Ease on the accelerator.

Tires spit gravel.

6:14 a.m., still somewhere in California desert, blasting through gears, lost in the unmistakable yet now-familiar airplane whistle of the Porsche engine, foot to the floor until the speedometer hits 90, effortless, then checking the rearview—clear—and backing off, pushing in Metallica cassette, the purple day standing still at 75. You hit PLAY.

You light a cigarette and crack the driver's window.

The tears stop, anger replacing fear, slamming the steering wheel with both hands. Then a slow wave of sick loneliness pushes away the anger. You want to cry. You want to puke. You want to dump the car in the desert and helicopter home. You want to be a normal person with a new life.

Not you.

Not now.

Not ever.

Soundtrack.

You adjust the rearview so you can see yourself, your eyes smeared mascara black.

Glancing back and forth, mirror to road.

Mirror, road.

A lifeless blob stares back.

So this is your life, Jet. This is your freedom.

One-in-three Papa Jet.

Papa Jet curled up on a gurney waiting to die.

Clock's ticking, young lady.

You squeeze your hand into a fist and swing at the mirror, knocking it out of whack, unable to look at that stupid face another second.

Chapter Twenty-Six

YOU'RE ROLLING IN *AMERICA'S RIDE* with the faint whisper of AC doing little to keep you cool. You push in a CD and crank the volume. Fast metal. Screaming lyrics. The aggression calms you. You think about what Rolle said.

Beautiful.

Now there's an adjective you don't hear much around 1321. At least not to describe you.

Fine.

Hot.

You're not a beautiful person.

When you feel yourself start to cry, you reach over and turn up the CD even louder. The massive subwoofers kick hard, and thundering guitar riffs rattle the van. You stare at the road and try to hold back your tears. You're not going to let yourself full-on blubber. Fifteen minutes later you're driving over the big speed bumps.

Silvercrest.

You check your eyes in the rearview to make sure you're not all smudged into a total Goth. Good, mascara where it should be. You look at the alien staring back at you, the stranger from another galaxy.

Fat cow.

Freak.

A product past its shelf date: one-in-three shot DNA and bolted.

Tomorrow night, wrap yourself in leather one more time and drive alone into the black desert.

Shut up.

Inside Silvercrest. Instead of Nick at the front desk there's a rail-thin woman with a dark tan on her face and lots of wrinkles. She has a nice smile and has you sign the visitors notebook. You write your name.

"Think he's probably asleep," she says, pulling the notebook toward her and writing the time next to your name: 8:12 p.m. "You know where?" Pointing.

You nod. "Yeah."

Other than a TV somewhere, Silvercrest is pretty quiet. You start down the hallway, which is empty, and glance in the mostly dark rooms as you pass. You stop at the door to Papa Jet's room and look in: lights out, Papa Jet on his back asleep with his mouth hanging open. You walk in and slide onto the folding metal chair next to his bed. Both the rails are up on the bed, but you slide your hand through and touch his bony white hand. Warm.

You're not sure where this comes from, but what you say is, "Grandpa, I mean, if you even are my grandpa." You take a deep breath and look around as though someone might be listening. The curtain between the two beds is pushed all the way to the wall, and the other mattress still sits bare.

Jet times two, no one else.

"If I tell you something... there's something I need to tell you. Not *you*, you know, but someone. I think. I don't know. This doesn't make any sense, does it?"

Silence.

"Anyway, I don't know for sure if you're who I hope you are. My grandpa. But I'm glad I got to meet you." You glance down and smile when you see the red cowboy hat sitting on the dresser where you left it. There's also a worn leather tobacco pouch, rolling papers and a few already rolled up nicely. Then you just start talking and tell him about Amsterdam and Dad and possible Dutch dads #1 and #2, the one-in-three odds that you share blood. You tell him about Mom and the Atlantic City flyer and the drunk phone call that led you here. You pull out a cigarette and, realizing you can't light it, roll it between your fingers as you talk.

"I miss Mom," you say, admitting it. "Dad, too. Whoever he is. Someone. Anyone. Like when do I just get to be a kid, you know? All this stuff, my choices. It's all connected. Maybe for attention, you know, like, hey, look, I'm alive here. Anyone care? Look at this crazy shit I'm doing. Anyone care? Hello, I'm stealing cars now. Anyone? I know I sound totally mental, right?"

The first time you've ever let the words come out of your head. The words and the truth out there now, somewhere in Papa Jet's brain, too. You look around to make sure no one else heard. You feel safe here with Papa Jet, some relief. You wait for something to happen, but nothing does. Then it's like slow motion, squeeze his hand, your other hand dropping the unlit cigarette and covering your mouth.

Too late, it's out there now.

Tears.

You pinch your lower lip and look at the cute little white whiskers on Papa Jet's chin. You speak in a voice so low that even if Papa Jet were awake he would have to strain to hear you. It's weird to hear yourself telling the story, Harrison West, California Dreaming or bust, Rolle, three weeks, ten cars, fifteen a pop. Number ten looming like a grizzly bear in the trees who just caught the sizzle of bacon fat.

God, you so need a cigarette right now. You pick up one of Papa Jet's hand-rolled, smelling it, sweet cherry tobacco, and then pinching it between your fingers. "So anyway, stupid me, you know, I don't want to get busted by the IRS, so I do what Jordan and Tina say. No bank account. No checking account. Cash only. Paid all my bills with money orders from the gas station. Basically kept everything in a gym bag at their studio. I know, Grandpa, stupid. Anyway, one night while we were out someone stole the bag. I'm pretty sure it wasn't my roomies, you know, like a set-up, but what's it matter anyway? I lost everything I'd saved. I had close to fifteen grand in that bag. I don't even know for sure how much. That was Jenna. Stupid Jenna. So when I came out here, 'Jet' was supposed to be smarter than that and, well, guess what?"

More quiet tears. Sniffles.

Everything pouring out now from some dark little corner, a place not so much in your mind but somewhere deeper that you've kept under close watch. You can actually feel yourself slipping into this space, endless, and if you tried to yell for help now nothing would come out, like in a silent nightmare. You curl into yourself and let go. A dull blackness is taking you away. You can't feel a thing. Numb. Everything numb. You squeeze yourself tight and cry, tucking your head into your chest, protecting you from something, searching for a safe place. You're not sure how long you go away, but it seems really quick. Then gradually, everything starts to come back in slow-motion waves. Your nose is all stuffed up from the crying. But you're breathing. Breathing is good. The Silvercrest disinfectant smell sort of wakes you back up to where you are again.

Breathe.

Breathe.

You feel spent, just crossed the finish line in a race you've been running your entire life and finally, at least in this moment, you get to rest. Somehow, after all the running and searching, holy shit, you're safe here in this black hole of agony nursing home with your one-in-three Papa Jet. You actually hear that voice in your head: *It's OK, Jet. You're safe here.*

You sniffle and dry your eyes. Your face is wet with tears, and by now your eyes must be a real mess. Total Goth for sure. You pull a tissue from the box on the dresser and blow your nose.

Awareness.

You are there.

Standing at the point of no return: You haven't ever trusted anyone... well, ever. Like *really* trusted someone. And then Papa Jet comes along and, grandpa or not, no reason to trust him, but you do. Well, sort of. He is asleep. But still, it's a start. Right? Then your mind flashes back to the beginning of the ride.

That's where you start, at the beginning, and as you talk you feel this weird mixture of fear and relief (but mostly relief), like you've needed to do this for a long time. Put down the giant boulder you've been carrying around your whole life. God, it feels good to just finally unload it all. Once you get started, your mouth can't keep up with your brain, like how you jump right in with Rolle to get away from Harrison, about how at first you really thought Rolle would be a good thing like how he never charged you rent, but how things changed three weeks ago with the cars.

You say how you've gone nine times no snags with just one more to go, stuck out there in the black desert with nothing but bad choices, how the set-up works with Bobby B, the valet operation, the pick-ups and drop points, the flight back to Phoenix with $15,000 cash shrink-wrapped.

Airport dogs.

Double-Blind, Two-Box Lock-Up.

You open your little purse and hold up the key to the money key. Then you tell him about number ten, one last ride lined up for 2 a.m. Monday morning, rad Porsche 911 Turbo owned by an oncologist with a post-modern glass-and-steel on a mountain. You take Papa Jet's hand again.

"Sounds stupid, but this feels like my one last chance to put my life back together." Then, never again.

No more escort.

No more boosting cars.

A normal person with a normal life.

Chapter Twenty-Seven

WHEN YOU BEGIN PASSING through the weird stretch of giant three-bladed white windmills, you know you've been on the road more than four hours. Both sides of the highway and up onto the hillsides: a sea of whirling propellers mounted on white poles tall as buildings. It's an eerie sight, like you're on a different planet. Soon the westbound lanes expand from two to four. Four lanes will mark the outer fringes of the insane urban sprawl that is Los Angeles. You'll be passing Beaumont, Calimesa and Riverside.

Once you pass San Bernardino, you want to begin a cautious celebration. You're really getting the feel of being in LA as the traffic thickens with each westbound on-ramp and the pace gets jacked up a few notches. You already feel safer here, less exposed. You're out of the desert now, in more ways than one, and can finally let yourself believe that your new life is about to begin. You open the sunroof and let the cool California air wash over you, how you're right in the middle of metro LA now, cruising past the exits for the 57 down to Fullerton.

You go one last time and end up here on number ten: rolling toward the ocean with 150 crisp C-notes on the back end when you park behind Dairy Queen and a Scotsman named Bobby B takes title.

Says how later today you'll walk off a plane at Sky Harbor in Phoenix and go straight to two different banks to divvy up.

Double-Blind, Two-Box Lock-Up.

$100,000 stacked cold.

You watch the back end of a big rig, take a deep breath, and squeeze the leather wheel. You try to push away all the hurdles you still have to clear. Just groove with the traffic flow and think about how close you are.

No hassles.

No cops.

No scares since Indio.

You pass the exit for the 605 freeway. You think about how weird it is you met Papa Jet and how he's been inserted into the equation of your new life. Good parts of your life always speeding by so fast you're like, what the hell just happened? You think about how far you've come since rolling onto I-10 in Phoenix almost six hours ago, how you survived the last lonely desert night of your life.

Never again.

You pass the exit for the San Diego Freeway, the 405, and wipe away some tears. You're so close now you can taste the salt in the ocean. Now the sign for Highway 1, the Pacific Coast Highway, end of the line for I-10. You give the horn two quick blasts and laugh as you signal right, whipping the crucial Porsche across two lanes of traffic like, hell yeah, look out world, nobody move.

Jet times one rolling west.

Exit Lincoln Boulevard and make a left.

Ten blocks down on the right is a Dairy Queen and behind the DQ is a garage. Bobby B is waiting for you right now in that garage with $15,000 shrink-wrapped.

Drop and run one last time, and you're free.

The freedom of $100,000.

Three weeks.

Ten times.

It all seems so easy now.

Yeah, right. Just shut up and drive.

When I-10 ends, you're in Santa Monica and work your way onto Ocean Avenue, cruising south with the sunroof and windows open, cool California breeze blowing in off the shimmering Pacific to your right.

But you won't relax until you drop keys into Bobby B's palm and walk away. Actually, you won't relax a bit until you're through airport security and at 35,000 feet headed east.

Speed Yellow slab of Stuttgart's finest rolling down a jammed Santa Monica street.

Fresh ocean air.

Papa Jet.

You think about how much time he has left.

Clock's ticking, young lady.

People are walking their dogs and Rollerblading and riding bikes along the walkway that winds through towering palm trees and lush grass that runs right to the cliff's edge. The view to the pier and beach and ocean below is spectacular. The smell is clean and fresh, moist ocean air taste in the back of your throat.

Then disinfectant.

You get a big Silvercrest whiff that makes your stomach turn.

You start to think the word.

The only word needed to describe what's going to happen to Papa Jet.

Soon.

Three weeks ago.

You push the word away before it can fully register in your brain.

Not him.

Please not now.

Not two days after you meet him.

Not ever.

Rolling up Wilshire and then right onto Lincoln. You pick up Rolle's directions from here: Ten blocks down on the right is the Dairy Queen. Traffic is heavy, but then again, you are in Southern California; traffic is always heavy. Lincoln Boulevard, even though it runs parallel to Ocean Avenue and is still Santa Monica, might as well be a different planet. Gone are the swaying palms and ocean vista and the laid-back California groove you felt moments ago. Lincoln Boulevard is urban intense: traffic and endless storefronts jammed side-by-side, and a feel that's gritty and chaotic and industrial. Perfect place to drop a hot $115,000 Porsche, because there's so much city churning noise no one will notice another dirty alley transaction.

You run it through your mind, Bobby B protocol, intense and friendly in a creepy sort of way and talking a million miles an hour in a Scottish accent that's barely intelligible.

Rolling in Santa Monica, clock running.

You refocus: drop ride and get back safe.

Dairy Queen straight ahead.

Five minutes away now from the last $15,000 shrink-wrapped and a lift back to LAX from Bobby B. You signal and pull into the Dairy Queen and then drive past the building to the garage you can already see.

Palms wet.

Heart racing.

Car-for-cash-drop-and-swap 60 seconds away.

The garage has two bays, with the doors closed on both. You wheel the Porsche in front of the rusted door on the right, scanning now for the little piece of paper with the red dot: Deal's Live. You can see the paper taped to the door, except the breeze has it flipped; you can't see the red dot. You glance in the rearview out of habit: directly behind you is Lincoln Boulevard, about 75 yards back.

No sign of any heat, just heavy traffic flashing back and forth across the gap between buildings.

You kill the engine and without thinking pull the key and climb out yelling, "Bobby B! Rock and roll, my friend, let's do this."

Your body is buzzing. You're actually here. Minutes away from being done forever.

Your hands are shaking.

Throat dry.

Where is he?

You rub your hands together and walk to the paper taped to the door, feeling a weird twinge that Bobby B hasn't shown his trademark sunburnt smile yet. Nine times prior he pokes his blistered little mug out within seconds of your arrival.

Starts running his hand along sleek German flares.

Giethehorn a weepamp.

But so far, nothing.

There it is again, weird twinge, something's not quite right here. You stop and turn again toward the road.

No one around.

A weird eerie silence here in the middle of the city, some sort of black hole sucking all the sound away. Basically, some bad juju about to break loose.

It's cool enough in the morning shade to goose-bump your arms.

Sleazy garage makes you feel sad and then angry at yourself for even being here. You feel so completely alone.

Cold and silent.

DQ's not open at 8:30 in the morning, and neither is this garage with a faded sign that says Manny's Auto.

"Bobby B?" You bang on the metal door with an open palm, and it rattles back and forth.

Nothing.

"Come on, stop messing around." Just as you say that, you flip the paper and choke on your own breath. Nine times straight you see a white sheet of paper with a red dot taped to the building. Today it's all gone wrong.

Today you see a green dot.

All bets off; heat's coming down from somewhere.

Clock's ticking, young lady.

You and Speed Yellow Sally are on your own.

What is happening here?

But before you can think the next thought or take a single step back toward the white-hot Porsche, you see something that freezes your entire universe.

Straight ahead.

Coming up slow in the narrow gap.

Black-and-white rolling this way.

Chapter Twenty-Eight

HERE'S THE FIRST THING YOU HEAR Papa Jet say at the horse track: Daily Double, wants the two horse in the first and the six horse in the second. You look down at Papa Jet. All these years. You feel a lump rise in your throat that moves slowly through your body and makes you smile. Standing here at the horse track under a thick haze of cigarette smoke, you feel normal. This outing was Nick Sands' idea, a little diversion for Papa Jet, who was as razor-sharp as anyone when it came to picking winning ponies. But ever since the stroke, according to Nick, that energy, passion and acumen came and went like a light being clicked on and off.

Out at the track with Papa Jet. You've barely known your would-be grandpa three days, and yet being here with him has a familiarity unlike any you've ever felt. Papa Jet is having a relatively good day, and is flipping pages in the program in which he spent all afternoon scribbling.

"Good breaker," Papa Jet says. "Likes the rail. Fades a little, but I think she'll be in the money. The Elias Stables. Trained in Louisiana. They sired couple of my old favorites: *VE Snappy Haircut* and *AZ Platinum Boy*."

He's talking to you, but mostly he's going back into his own mind and conversing with a younger version of himself. "Amazing. Closer. She was the best."

You look at the name of the four horse: *Jean Paul's Special*.

"Needs. Get out. Four hole fast."

"Oh yes, I think she will," you say, not quite sure how he knows all this.

"That horse is...," he says, coughing. "Bloodline. Look at the way she breaks. Then she'll get on that rail and run... the wind."

You pull out a $100 bill. "Let's bet it like we don't care if we lose it," you tell him. "No scared money here." You wink at Papa Jet and wheel him to the betting window.

Horse track people use the number; you're all about the names. You look at Papa Jet studying the program, surrounded by clinking glasses and chatter and the incessant whine of a loudspeaker. He's immersed in the racing program.

Sarina Dancer Shake Shake

JD's Go Sexy Jetson.

AR Flexible Gemini.

You watch the jockeys loading the horses for the first race. Listening to Papa Jet talk horses reminds you of Rolle talking cars. Then the metal gates fly open and the horses are on the track. You and Papa Jet are sitting near a cocktail lounge that's so smoky your eyes burn. You're leaning your elbows on a sticky table and watching the race on a TV monitor. You can't even see the actual track from this back corner, which Papa Jet chose for its proximity to the betting window.

"Come on four. Come on."

Jean Paul's Special breaks out and is already in first place when the pack hits turn one. "She's winning! She's winning." You look at Papa Jet and all the scribbles on his program. Out of turn two *Jean Paul's Special* has stretched the lead to two lengths over the eight horse, which has a yellow-and-black-striped blanket. Your four horse is in green. The color of money. Turn four and onto the final straightaway and *Jean Paul's Special* is running away from the pack, eight lengths now, nine, ten. You're cheering and so is Papa Jet, leaning forward in his wheelchair and repeating, "Go. Go. Go. Go." The light comes on and the camera photographs the finishing order, with *Jean Paul's Special* the winner by 12 lengths. Papa Jet smiles and hands you a stack of betting slips as he turns his attention to the second race.

"Should I go cash these in?" you ask.

"Go ahead, dear," Papa Jet says, his eyes never leaving the page. You walk to the window and hand the stack of tickets to the attendant, who runs them one by one through a slot in the machine.

Total payout: $379.

After the big start, Papa Jet's luck runs cold other than one race where he picks a black horse named *White Mountain Vortex* that gets on the rail and digs hard. Start to finish, and Papa Jet had him all the way because he liked the bloodline.

By the ninth race, Papa Jet is slumped in his wheelchair with his cowboy hat pulled low over his eyes and his head down. You stand behind him and rub his shoulders for another race that he barely watches. The optimism you had when your night at the races started is gone. You feel sad and alone again. Even with the big payout, the $100 you fronted has become $46. But you're certain in his mind tomorrow, when he recalls the night, he will relay the story of the big payout led by *Jean Paul's Special* that will grow to $400 or $500.

"Ready to go?" you ask.

He barely nods. You push Papa Jet through the sea of tired faces, smoke burning your eyes, and down the long, low ramp that eventually leads you outside. The night's hot, 100-plus easy, but the oven blast feels good because it gets you out of the smoke. You walk across hot asphalt until you're pushing Papa Jet through the gate and into the parking lot. The euphoria of going ten times and getting your money has given way to this bigger reality. Once he's tucked in back at Silvercrest, you'll drive back to Las Palmas. Papa Jet times one alone at Silvercrest.

Time is for you.

Time is against you.

You stop pushing the wheelchair, lean down and hold Papa Jet closer than you've ever held anyone. And then you cry.

You cry for a long time.

Chapter Twenty-Nine

YOU DON'T KNOW EXACTLY HOW it all happens so fast. First the standoff, black-and-white stopping, cop running plate. Then red and blue flashes of the inevitable rolling this way: piss luck trickling through the grate.

Kill or be killed.

Diving toward the car and thinking, good thing the ignition's on the left like Rolle said.

Left hand buries laser-cut key in dash hole while right hand grabs wheel.

Terror. Thundering waves charge through your entire body in dark flashes, surges of adrenaline so maniacally pure you've lost control of your own mind.

Brain and body and blood blurring into white-hot panic.

Autopilot.

This is serious. This is how the end happens, swift, clinical, chopped down in a single 60-second block. Guillotine blade severing bone and life.

Car moving, but who's driving?

Engine screaming, tachometer gobbles red as you spin the import around.

Heading straight at the black-and-white now.

Your foot.

Your foot is heavy to the floor, Porsche rocketing forward at a speed you know should be terrifying, but you don't feel a thing. Numb. Everything numb out there somewhere.

Breathe.

Breathe.

You're breathing again. The oxygen is back.

A long, loud car horn blast snaps you awake, Porsche spinning sideways across Lincoln. Cars and trucks swerving. Screeching rubber sounds that make you wince. Speed Yellow 911 cutting a clean swath of asphalt through a maze of metal. Jet head times one jerked right when the ass-end of Stuttgart's finest stops dead.

Pause.

Engine idling.

Chaos all around.

Rearview.

Black-and-white nosing into heavy traffic with lights flashing.

Your mind demanding an answer as to how exactly you got all the way across this road without hitting anything?

Awareness.

Rearview: black-and-white flashing red and blue and cutting this way across Lincoln. LAPD mainframe times one chewing Arizona plate and coming back stolen if the oncologist punched digits.

Felony charge.

Grand theft auto times ten.

Radio for backup.

Clock's ticking, young lady.

The entire LAPD looking to snag the babe in the little German sports car. Your entire life compressed into a million random images that burst before you in a single flash. One cleansing thought.

You are not a car thief, official or otherwise, unless you get caught.

Porsche Tiptronic S: thumb-shift your way to freedom.

Then the flashbulb goes dim, and you punch the accelerator and blast your way north on Lincoln. Except you forget about the 420 muscled German ponies that have been doing the equivalent of tethered kiddie rides since you rolled out of Phoenix early this morning.

It's dangerous to forget about 420 muscled German ponies.

Precision German steeds flexing their collective power in unison as you weave and scream through traffic in first gear. Just like Rolle said, enough torque in second gear at 65 mph to pick the left front wheel off the ground while the other three wheels chew California asphalt. You forget about the top track speed of 185. You forget you never dropped $3,000 on high-performance driving school to learn how to handle what amounts to a race car. You forget all this, and in the span of seconds, the car pimp slaps your brain.

You never even get to second gear before the car lurches to the right, even though you didn't aim it that way, and starts to spin. Now you're headed straight toward the back end of a huge delivery truck that's stopped in traffic, so you panic and yank the wheel back hard left, over-correcting.

Except car computer times one kicks in—WRONG, DUMB-ASS—and corrects your misjudgment. The oil stains and morning ocean moisture on Lincoln Boulevard have other ideas, too, and send you straight north in a 360-degree spin. Minus the computer you would have buried the car into the delivery truck. Somehow you miss everything else in your path.

When you finally stop, the nose of the Porsche is pointed south, back the way you came, hands on wheel in a death-grip, your heart pumping wildly as you watch two cop cars now heading straight toward you with balls-out reds and blues.

Deep breath.

Then without hesitation you punch the accelerator again and spin the car back north and race up Lincoln Boulevard. None of this seems real: racing through Santa Monica in a stolen 911 with two cops now in pursuit. You've seen car chases a million times in the movies, so in a disconnected way you've already been here. You've also played this scene out nine times before, working the scenarios in your mind and how you'd out-drive the heat like you're Wonder Woman or something. But now it's real, and the reality doesn't match the movies you ran in your head.

In reality, everything's coming at you from the driver's perspective, the world whipping toward you low and fast and chaotic, blurred, which is a lot different from the bird's-eye chases in your mind.

No time to think or react.

Just drive.

And try not to crash.

You blast back under I-10, sirens wailing, flashing lights still filling rearview. Red stoplight ahead. Colorado Avenue.

You grab one gear lower with your right thumb, tach digging right like a hungry wolf on a fresh bone, and brake before entering the intersection. Even so, you blow the red light at 80 and, somehow, slice through unscathed. You cringe when, staring in the rearview, you see the rear cop car get clipped crossing Colorado and spun around in a wicked 360. This whole thing has moved to the insanity level, but you can't stuff the glue back in the tube now. The only way out is to dig yourself in deeper and pray. Now you're all in, push the stack to center and try to beat the track before the track beats you.

When you get to Wilshire, you have to slow down more because the traffic is so heavy, grabbing two gears lower and barely missing a banged-up El Camino, the pissed-off driver cranking hard left to avoid you and smashing into a gleaming black Mercedes.

"Sorry," you say sheepishly to the rearview. You would die if someone got hurt because of you. Maybe it's time to stop the madness, just surrender.

As that thought lingers you steer around the carnage and continue your run north on Lincoln, whipping around cars, swerving in and out of oncoming traffic. When you grab a quick glance in the rearview, you can see you've gained some distance on the single cop car flashing red and blue. But instead of being a good thing, your panic deepens: Rolle always told you that outrunning chase cars, especially in LA, won't do you any good. Soon as a chase starts pursuers are trained, and required, to radio for support and back off so people don't get hurt. Then the helicopters go up. A little distance between the car chasing you means nothing. You know there's already backup units getting a bead on you and stretching spiked chains across the road that will blow all your tires. If the bird's not already up, it will be in minutes. This is a game you won't win.

Clock's ticking, young lady.

What you've got to do now, Rolle's words in your head, is deploy evasive driving tactics. The clock started as soon as the chase began. You only have a few minutes to get out of sight before the birds are locked onto you. Once the helicopter's got you, you're on the next episode of COPS. So get yourself in a neighborhood and lose them before they can get a solid fix on your position. Then get the car off the road and out of sight. Think parking garage. Underpass. An alley with an open garage. All you're looking to do is dump the car, anything to put you out of helicopter vision, and get out on foot. Then wipe down the rig, walk away and consider it off limits for good. You walk clean, you don't want to ever be within five miles of that ride again.

With that in mind, you pull a hard right onto a smaller side street and gun it, then another right, screaming down a residential street in second gear at 80 miles an hour. Out of nowhere, a group of kids are suddenly chasing a ball into the middle of the street. Right in your path. Your brain flashes: shouldn't they be in school?

Lock your arms.

Slam both your feet onto the brake pedal and dig in as hard as you can.

Jet seat belt times one locking up.

Kids times too many right in your path.

Car computer and internally vented, cross-drilled brakes take control—WHO IS THIS DUMB-ASS DRIVING?—and keep the Porsche from spinning out of control. Kids scattering except a little girl completely frozen on asphalt.

You stop dead, no skid.

Jet head times one snapped back into the headrest. You're stopped so close to the little girl you can't see her bottom half.

Two-hands-to-mouth terror.

"Oh my God, oh my God."

Kid crying now. You instinctively unbuckle and open your door. Then a voice, she's OK, she's OK. You gotta go.

You look at the screaming little girl, whose face is red and wet with tears. You know the voice is right. She's OK, just scared. And you're down to your last few 60-second blocks before the chop and swoop of helicopter blades signals your final death knell. You yell out how sorry you are to the little girl before slamming your door and going into Reverse, the street lined on both sides with parked cars. You can't get around with her in the street.

An open driveway.

You thumb-shift and wheel into the driveway, then a hard left onto the sidewalk and back out the other side at the next open driveway, little girl still frozen and crying in the rearview. You can see a main road just to your left.

Heart racing.

Palms completely soaked. Then you remember the emergency phone number Bobby B gives you each time you drop. He changes the number constantly, a brick cell he said he will personally answer if the wheels come off. You're thinking, yeah, the wheels have definitely come off. Then you hear a siren that builds and then fades. You won't let yourself believe you just out-drove the cops. You won't believe that until you're sitting with Papa Jet back at Silvercrest for afternoon bingo. You'd give anything to smell Silvercrest disinfectant right now.

Standstill in Santa Monica, clock running.

You need to call Bobby B for help.

You pull up to the stop sign, slowly, and then stop at Wilshire. No sirens. No cops in sight. No police birds overhead. Not yet at least.

"Maybe," you say, still cautiously looking left and right. A loud horn blast gives you a near-fatal heart attack, truck grille filling rearview, a driver back there yelling. You turn left onto Wilshire and head east. Pay the ugly tax this one last time, please God, and you swear you'll walk away clean. No more. Never again. Please just let you get back to Phoenix in one piece, and you're done.

Eyes scanning for cop cars and a parking garage or somewhere safe to ditch the Hot Wheels. You hang a right on Bundy. You know generally where you are, but you have no idea where you're going. You see an airplane and feel a wave of panic, certain they're coming to get you. But it's just a private plane that banks left away from you. Complete paranoia has set in now.

"Shit, there's no way I'm getting out of this. No way." You turn onto a side street and pull into the parking lot of a closed video store with a big sign: "Be Kind. Please Rewind."

Trembling.

Engine idling.

You dig in your purse and light a Marlboro. Something to settle the nerves and your shaking hands. You take a long pull. A few nervous puffs that aren't doing shit to calm you. What the hell are you going to do?

Maybe you should just wipe the car clean right here and walk away. You let out the smoke.

Quick breaths, waiting for some kind of plan to surface.

But nothing does.

And you have no earthly idea what your next move should be.

Chapter Thirty

YOU FEEL MORE VULNERABLE and exposed and scared than you ever have on any six-hour desert run. Eyes ahead and rearview, back and forth. Thumbs at the ready in case you need to make another run for your life. Scanning side to side, too.

The words roll through your head. No more. Never again. Just let this turn out right, and that's it. You hear a chopper and lean forward to watch it move above you, close enough that you can see it's LAPD. Your body tenses. You lean back and see the helicopter in the rearview and watch it continue away from you. This could induce a heart attack.

Then you're rolling into the first gas station you see and parking under the awning by the pumps for cover. The pay phones are across the parking lot by the store. You get lots of long, silent stares from the group of teenagers smoking in front of the store. You kill the engine.

You jump out of the car, and as you near the store you hear a few whistles and some comments about you and the car. You have to actually stop and say "Excuse me" to cut through the kids to the phones. They mostly look bored, not dangerous, but their proximity to the phone is unsettling. You plug in coins and punch Bobby B's numbers. He answers after one ring. Even when he says a single word you can hear the unmistakable Scottish brogue: "Yeah?"

"It's me. What the hell?" No names, he told you first time he gave you the number. You're on Olympic, traffic heavy, the morning haze casting an eerie gray chill. The smell of grit and smog is pressing in all around you. Kids staring.

"I'll explain later, but some daft wanker snitched us out, and now the heat's coming down everywhere. Drop points. Pier. Safe house. We're skint. We're trying to sneak one last shipment out before we go into hibernation mode. Still got the package?"

"Yeah, it's here with me." You look back toward the car, but your view's blocked by the milling teenagers and the gas pumps. Even with your jacket on, you're shivering in the cool air.

"Brilliant, ye are, pure dead brilliant. I was worried about you. Wipe the package and walk away. Afraid this one's D.O.A., luv."

"Hold on, no, no, no; I need to get rid of this. I'm stuck at a gas station in Santa Monica and getting chased——"

"Luv, we're fucking skint. Wipe the package and walk away. Count yer dosh from the others and——"

"OK, you'll meet me with the money?"

Silence.

"Hello?"

"Right cheeky bird you are. It's no worth it, luv. Walk away."

"I am. And then you're giving me my money. Right?"

"Sorry, luv, we folded up shop, and everyone's scattered from here to there. It's D.O.A. It's no just you, the whole thing's come apart. We're finished. Ratted out and under the bright white light for sure."

Why is this happening? You'll never get what's yours from Rolle if you don't get this money now. "Bobby, please, I'll leave the, you know, package here. Send someone to pick it up later. Please, I need that money."

"Luv, that's no how it works. What you've got there is tainted, pure and simple. Toxic like."

"Look, toxic like or not I did my end, right? So now it's your turn: tell me where you are so I can come get my money."

Silence.

The kids shuffle around a bit and you look back toward the Porsche. You just say, "Please..."

Silence.

"For fuck's sake, even if I wanted do this for you it's no going to matter. There's no enough time."

"Yes there is. I'll come meet you. That's it."

"For fuck's sake… It'll no work, but if you want to try…"He lets out a deep sigh."I'm a daft bastard for doing this. Only for a right tidy bird like you would I make this exception; you get to me I'll pay you anyway. But you dump the package right there. Don't go near it, OK? We clear on that, luv?"

"Got it."

"But make sure you wipe it clean first."He says it again louder: "Make sure you wipe it clean."

"Wipe it clean. Got it." Except you look around your immediate vicinity: the group of teenagers, six or seven cars at the pumps, people in and out of the store with sodas and newspapers and coffee cups. Traffic flashing by on the street. Not exactly the best fingerprint-wipe-down venue.

"Bobby?"

"Yeah luv?"

"What if I can't do what you just said? What then?"

"Well, you have to because when they find it your prints will be all over it."

"OK, I'll see what I can do."

"But even if you do that, you'll no make it to me before I leave."

"Leave? Where are you going?"

"I'm disappearing, luv. Remember that certain animal I warned you about?"

Animal? What's he——and then you remember.

Money-sniffing dogs looking to take you down.

LAX.

Bobby B's at the airport ready to blow the country.

"I know exactly where you are. Same as before?"

"No bad. Smart wee bird."

Wipe the car and walk away clean. Get Jet times one to LAX to pick up $15,000. Fly back to Phoenix and collect. Game over.

"OK, where then?"you ask.

"I'm looking at a McDonald's. But this'll no work, luv. There's no time."

"Shut up, yes there is," you say. You figure with wiping it down, getting a cab and even though you're not that far from the airport, L.A. traffic… an hour should cover you. "I'll be there inside an hour."

Silence.

"Hello? Did you hear me?"

"I'm sorry luv. It'll no work."

"Why?"

You don't really want to hear his answer. Then he says, "You have half that time, and then I'm gone for good."

Chapter Thirty-One

YOU THINK ABOUT HOW MUCH TIME you have left. Thirty minutes and then a lifetime of freedom. You think about how much time Papa Jet has left.

Clock's ticking, young lady.

"I'll be there," you say, hanging up, everything moving in slow-motion. Ideally, you'd just wipe the car clean and leave it at that gas pump. But not with all those kids watching and wondering, what the hell?

You glance at your watch: 28 minutes. Straight to the airport, ditch the car and then meet your guy at McDonald's. But how?

Watch: 27 minutes.

The morning is still gray. All you're looking for is a quick place to dump the car and go. But you're boxed in here. Traffic's thicker now, slowing and grinding along, stop-and-go, 15-miles-an-hour. Then you miss a few breaths when you see a cop rolling into the gas station and sitting back behind the pumps. You slide behind the bank of pay phones. Shit, shit, shit. Did they get a make on you back there? Computer chewing Arizona plate and coming back hot if he sees you over here. You're in the shark's jaw, nowhere to hide now.

Cop stopped but no closer to you. You're far enough away over here he can't see you, but you can't waste any more time hiding. Clock's ticking. Now the cop car moving again, closing in.

Watch: 24 minutes.

Now you're moving slowly, but this is not good. Maybe slide across the front of the store and duck behind. Just get the hell out of here. Cop pulling alongside the Porsche now. Holy crap. It's happening. You're certain your mug is visible now and those red and blue lights are going to flash any second. Now you're afraid to move away from the safety of the pay phones. No escape. You close your eyes, take a deep breath and peek again.

Bingo.

Cop one on the radio, Johnny Law taking title now of the Speed Yellow slab.

Watch: 23 minutes.

Critical minutes slipping away.

Heart racing.

Hands wet.

This will never work. Decision: leave the hot package covered with your fingerprints, or drive, clean and dump it elsewhere?

Normal twentysomething people will never encounter this choice.

Then you hear your death sentence, the loud chop of helicopter blades. You lean forward and, of course, a chopper off to your right headed this way and hovering so close you can practically see the mean stare in the pilot's eyes.

You take a breath and try to slow things down a bit, one last time to weigh your options to beat the clock:

Walk away and call a taxi. *You're in LA, not Manhattan. It's not like you can flag a cab and be on your way inside 30 seconds. Waiting for a taxi might chew up half your time or more. Plus there's the problem of leaving the car unwiped. No good.*

Wipe the car and pay someone to drive you. *OK, assuming you can wipe the car, Reginald Clifton Rolle always makes you take $500 cash that he calls the Emergency Mishap Fund. Then who? Those loitering teenagers over there? Great, there's seven witnesses to your crime. Too many loose lips. A random passerby? Same problem: loose end in LA.*

Every scenario you conjure involves other people, which makes you very nervous: pay someone to wipe down the car (maybe those boys), pay them to drive it around the corner for you, etc. No good.

Walk away and go home. *Convince Rolle to divvy up $135,000. Tell him he can keep his end at $50,000 and you'll take $85,000. This seems the safest and most logical solution: Rolle gets his either way. But there's one glaring loose end here, too: Rolle's repeated threats of indentured servitude if you don't finish the deal. Although he'd never admit it, on some level he knows once you finish this deal, you're gone. If you don't finish, then he'd have a bargaining chip to keep you around. And you have no doubt he'd writeoff his $50K if he got to keep you instead. Worst-case, if it really went sour, he'd bury his money key in a Dumpster in another state just to spite you. You suspect this was never fully about the money for Rolle: This has been an adrenaline thrill ride as much as anything. If you don't finish what you started and divvy back in Phoenix, it will likely all be for nothing. No good.*

Get in the car and go. Wipe as you drive and walk clean at the airport. *That's the dumbest idea you've ever had. Even dumber than agreeing to this entire scenario in the first place. This last option isn't even open for consideration. So shut up already. LA mainframe chewing plate number. Swarms of cops scouring asphalt. Would you really consider trading $100,000 for felony jail time? Or, another way to look at it: a 20-minute drive, and then you're done for good.*

deep wicked freaky.

Says how you're always forced into making one more bad decision to undo all the other bad decisions. Says how everything gets real fuzzy in your head as the seconds tick away.

Barter it.

Sell it.

Give it away.

Congratulations, it's a girl.

Congratulations, it's a girl.

Congratulations, it's a girl.

Says how just once you'd like to finish something right in your life and get what you deserve, even if that's the most twisted thing you've ever heard.

Says how you told Rolle there's no way you'd ever drive a stolen car to California. And ten? Forget it. Not worth the risk. You're not a car thief, official or otherwise, unless you get caught.

Says how you'd be the runner, first link in the chain that moves late-model imports from Phoenix to LA, a six-hour blast give or take.

Says how all you need to know is that every time you drop a freaky-hot ride in LA, you fly back to Phoenix fifteen total, ten to the good. That's tall cash, baby, shrink-wrapped in plastic.

You were all, tall cash?

Fifteen thousand dollars.

Fifteen thousand?

In six hours.

Six hours?

Six hours.

That is a golden egg.

That's what I'm sayin.

Says how Rolle's not here now, and the new deal goes like this: one hundred thousand dollars.

One hundred thousand?

In 20 minutes.

20 minutes?

20 minutes.

*That is **the** golden egg.*

That's what we're sayin', Jet.

Clock's ticking, babe.

So you got the game to keep it together and stay cool?

Chapter Thirty-Two

IN SECONDS MORE COP CARS will be swarming you. Chopper closing fast. You're back on Lincoln driving toward your freedom. In the half-second before you hear the screeching rubber and a metal-on-metal crunch you think, almost there. The metal-on-metal crunch is the sound of a Porsche 911 getting clipped in the rear and spun out on Lincoln.

Everything is over before you have time to react.

Speed Yellow 911 at a standstill, half on the sidewalk. Your brain's all... huh? Foggy.

You glance left. Driver coming out of a black Chevy pickup with giant tires.

You see it all happening, and you're thinking you should be doing something because that dude's walking this way pretty fast.

A big guy, muscle-big not fat-big, thirty-something with a goatee and a black bandanna on his head. His dark blue work shirt, untucked and greasy. For some reason, your brain realizes this is the kind of guy Rolle told you about, last link in the food chain, parts dipped in solvent and sold to auto shops to resell as new.

After someone like you boosts a car.

And drops with someone like Bobby B who sells to someone who chops who sells to someone like this guy coming at you right now. In a single flash your brain sees an old lady walking out of the grocery store to an empty parking space. Standing there slack-jawed, brown sacks in each arm. How she spends the next 20 minutes confused and trying to figure out where she parked. Takes a long time for her to believe someone like you snagged her wheels right there in broad daylight while she was buying groceries to cook dinner for her fat grandson.

No one gets hurt.

Except what about that length of black pipe in this guy's right hand?

"No!" you scream, your brain snapping everything back to real time just as you see him raise the black pipe and yell something, your body instinctively diving down across the passenger seat.

BOOM, driver's-side window exploding inward and showering you with little glass chunks, now a big hairy arm coming through the window toward you.

"Stupid bitch."

Slow-motion.

Staring at his black bandanna, the way he looks at you with his three-day stubble, your eyes darting back and forth between his face and the steering wheel. He's shaking his head, sizing you up and playing it out in his mind. You know the look, same one the cop shot you this morning out on that black highway. You reach up and instinctively turn the key in the ignition. Except engine already running, starter grinding.

He just stares at you with that look, goose bumps on your arms, your brain going, this guy is as big as a Clydesdale horse but has no chance against 420 German ponies.

Then back to real time.

You reach your right foot up and push gas pedal to the floor, thumb-shift, German ponies kicking in, half of this dude in the car as you speed forward.

Both his arms in the car, black pipe swinging. Screaming. You press yourself all the way across the passenger seat.

Without slowing, you cut a wicked hard right, which catapults the dude around, his legs hitting the front body flare, the little squares of glass sliding around in the Porsche cockpit.

Then you slam on internally vented, cross-drilled brakes, and the dude is gone except for the blood he leaves on the seat and driver's door.

Holy shit. A purified jolt of Jet adrenaline.

Your brain isn't sure what to say or do or think. And what about that LAPD chopper?

Seconds thunder by in slow-motion, time frozen away in a cryogenic tube, the dude just ahead on the street by the front passenger wheel, but you're not sure if he's out cold, or just bloodied and regrouping. Without saying anything, you thumb-shift into Reverse and floor it, then slam brakes when you can see the dude pushing himself up onto his hands and knees.

You gun the flat-six a few times to send the dude a turbo wakeup call, special delivery. He pushes himself up onto one knee with his other leg straight out. "Think you broke my ankle." He's still struggling to stand, dragging his bad leg.

You feel horrible.

No one gets hurt.

Your thumb finds First with one click, then your foot punches the accelerator to the floor and cuts another hard left and you're southbound on Lincoln before the dude has a chance to yell another word. The cool air is rushing in the smashed window.

You check for cuts.

Nothing.

You feel sick that you hurt that guy back there. You reassure yourself that he'll be OK.

Watch: 21 minutes.

You're scanning for the chopper, but nothing. No cruisers in sight, either. The entire LAPD locked in on Jet times one as the eventual charges pile up. Add "hit-and-run" and "vehicular assault" to grand theft auto and high-speed craziness.

Every one of the next minutes of your life feels like hours and days of isolated torture. Heart thumping. Palms soaked. Eyes flashing road-to-rearview in a scattered blur.

Watch: 20 minutes.

Watch: 19 minutes.

Watch: 18 minutes.

The tension is too much. You can't do it. Just pull over, wipe clean and walk away. Road curving, 26 cop cars lined up now and waiting for you.

Clear the turn.

No cops in sight.

Watch: 17 minutes.

Then the helicopter chop again, distant, but slowly getting louder. You lean forward and strain for any view of the bird ready to take you down. Nothing.

CHAPTER THIRTY-TWO

Heart thumping double time.

Throat parched.

Speed Yellow slab a giant neon target on black LA asphalt.

Watch: 16 minutes.

Helicopter chop louder and louder, except no sight of it yet. Then you think, maybe they're following you, radar lock on brunette wrapped in buttery leather.

Watch: 15 minutes.

You swallow back the fear and try to breathe, but you're not sure if you are. Traffic starting to thicken, forcing you slow to 40, 35, 28. Agony.

Watch: 14 minutes.

LA gawkers slowing to look at a truck pulled to the side of the road, hood up, engine ablaze, flames lapping skyward. Rubberneck slowdown.

Then you see the red and blue flashes of a Highway Patrol cruiser.

Eyes front and center, missy.

Get those hands up.

What you need, missy, is to learn how to respect the law. And out here, I'm the law. And if I'm the law, we both know what that makes you. You ready to go to school?

Then you realize there are actually two cruisers, tail-to-nose behind the burning truck, officers milling around waving traffic along and setting up orange cones.

Helicopter chop directly above now, and you let out a nervous laugh of relief as you see it's a news team. Truck Ablaze Near LAX: Film at 11.

As you near the bottleneck, you can see they're waving cars into a single lane.

Three cops on point as each car rolls by at five miles an hour. There's no way out except forward, and the way forward is taking you right into the sticky web.

This is it.

The end of your run.

Just 12 minutes from glory.

Chapter Thirty-Three

AS YOU APPROACH THE STOP-AND-GO APEX, there's nothing you can do except try not to vomit and/or pee yourself. Both are distinct and likely possibilities in the next seconds.

Officers waving, truck blazing away.

A black truck takes its turn through the opening and then it's all you. Cops waving, glancing, watching the blaze, attention dispersed in multiple directions.

Jedi mind tricks: You don't need to bother with this Speed Yellow slab of Stuttgart's finest, just wave it and the cute driver right on through to the other side.

Rolling, rolling.

Five miles per hour.

Then eye contact with the cop, somehow turning his head just as you roll up. No smile, no nothing, just an intent glare from Johnny Law.

Now where you headed?

And just like that you're past the slowdown, accelerating and moving again toward your new life.

When you start seeing the signs for LAX, you're down to 9 minutes. By the time you're backing into a parking space (to hide the license plate), you can feel your new life slipping away.

Watch: 4 minutes.

There's no way you make it now.

Then you get a thought that makes you sick: How accurate is your timekeeping? Bobby B says 30 minutes, but you never synchronize, and maybe he only waits 24 or 25 minutes. In other words, maybe he's already gone. You still have to wipe the car and get inside to find Bobby B. While all those thoughts rip through your head, you're already out and wiping down the Porsche with one of your white socks: door handles, trunk area, gas tank. Anywhere that might have your prints. Bandanna-man smashed up the rear end pretty bad, the right taillight assembly shattered.

Big snags on number ten.

Then, because you're not exactly sure how hard you have to wipe glossy Speed Yellow to erase fingerprints, you wipe everything again.

Watch: 3 minutes.

"No, no, no," you say, "You're OK. Let's go." You start jogging and glance back at the car, let out a deep sigh of relief, and as you look back once more you run a final mental checklist:

Prints wiped.

Personal items removed.

Nothing to tie you or Rolle or anyone else back in Arizona to that car. Nothing, that is, except the Arizona plate that will lead LAPD to the oncologist on Camelback Mountain, pace tracks already burned into his deep-pile Berber as he awaits any news.

Clean drop, Jet. You're free!

Double down and try to beat the casino before the casino beats you.

Watch: 2 minutes.

You swivel around and break into a run toward the international terminal, one glance back, a weird pang of emotion as you walk away from what got you here in one piece, unscathed, safe.

Number ten kicked some serious ass.

Weird, but you nod to yourself and thumbs-up the German engineers back in Stuttgart. Then you're in an all-out run.

Chapter Thirty-Four

AT THE ROAD TO CROSS INTO THE TERMINAL, there's a crowd of people waiting for the crosswalk light to go green.

Watch: 1 minute.

You push through the people and then onto the first lane of the wide street. A bus swerves and narrowly misses you, people yelling, the bus horn blaring.

"Sorry, sorry," is all you can say as you cross the street, now two cars slamming their brakes and skidding, horrible shrieks of rubber on asphalt.

Horns blasting.

A loud crash from behind as one of the stopped cars gets rear-ended and hurtles forward into the crosswalk behind you, the sound making you jump and run faster.

No one gets hurt, except carnage in your wake keeps stacking up.

You find the safety of the sidewalk, through and then around a huge group of Japanese people with a mountain of luggage in your path. You steal a glance at your watch as you hit the automatic doors into the terminal.

Watch: 0 minutes.

"Bobby B, you better wait. You wait for me, you sunburnt little Scot."

Once inside, you pause to get your bearings, hands shaking, heart racing. You can see the meet-up point from here. You start through the mobs of people. Pushing, stopping, bumping into luggage, starting, stopping.

Watch: minus 1 minute.

It's a small McDonald's, so it's easy to see: no Bobby B.

You have half that time, and then I'm gone for good.

This can't be how it ends. Somehow. Some way. You check every person's face again—seated, standing, paper-hatted workers—no Bobby B. You yell "No!" so loud it stops conversations and draws a few stares. "Sorry." Then your gaze moves all the way to the security checkpoint.

Says how you see a small, wiry man in a full-length black leather coat and black beret. Even though you can't see anything but the back, you know immediately it's him just by his size and the way he's standing.

You're in a full-out sprint when you see him step through the metal detector and onto the other side of your new life.

You rush to the front of the line and start to yell his name, before he slips away for good, and then stop yourself realizing you're surrounded by security guards and police and federal agents. You can still see him, right there on the other side of the metal detector, loading his pockets back up. You wave frantically, but his attention is elsewhere. He turns and starts to walk into the terminal. You have maybe three seconds to get his attention, or it's over.

"Bobby! Bobby! Bobby B!"

It's the third "Bobby B" that stops him in his tracks, where he pauses and then, being the shrewd career criminal he is, doesn't turn or react or acknowledge you. He just starts walking again.

"Bobby B! It's me, Jet. Come back. Please. It's me, Jet!"

The last thing you yell stops him again on the other side. Two more steps, and he disappears around the corner forever. The last thing you yell also draws the attention of two uniformed security officers who are now in your face.

"Ma'am, you're going to need to stop yelling and step over here, please."

"OK, I'm OK. I thought that was someone I knew. Thank you."

"Ma'am," the other one says, "please step over here." Except now he's gripping your left arm hard enough that it hurts. And when you look up again, Bobby B is gone.

Game over.

And now you're really going down when these two connect you to the mayhem you caused coming in here, all of which was no doubt caught on camera. You're pretty hard to miss causing traffic pileups. You feel the tears start to come as the cops move you to the other side near a long table with more cops milling around. You came so close. Within a single 60-second block of meeting Bobby B. Ten times across the desert all comes down to seconds.

Rolle always said baseball is a game of inches and seconds. Just like life.

A few more seconds for $100,000.

"What was that all about?" one of the officers is asking you. "Do you have some ID?"

You can hear and see it all happening, but you just stare, unable to move.

"Ma'am? Your ID?"

Shouldn't you be doing something? Or saying something? But what did he just ask? Truthfully, could someone please explain what's happening right now?

Anyone?

"My luv, there you are. I was so worried."

It's a voice that sounds vaguely familiar, but not one you entirely recognize. When you turn and see Bobby B in his full-length black leather coat and black beret walking toward you, something's not quite right. His voice. He's doing a perfect American voice. Not even a hint of gie-the-horn-a-wee-pamp brogue.

"Excuse me officers; Dr. Reynolds. I've been looking all over for my wife here, and if she appeared panicked it's because we got separated and she needs her medication."

The officers move aside as Bobby B steps up, unscrewing the lid on a plastic amber bottle and handing it to his new wife. Then he pulls a bottle of water from his jacket pocket, breaks the seal and hands that to Jet.

"Go ahead. Everything's OK now."

"Thank you," you say. "Thank you, Dr. Reynolds."

"Never did like to call me by my first name," Bobby B says, laughing and covering your gaffe with an Oscar-worthy performance. The voice is uncanny. "All these years calling me Dr. Reynolds instead of just 'Burt.'"

"Your name's Burt Reynolds?" one of the cops asks.

Bobby B nods, "I know. No relation."

This is unbelievable.

"Feeling better?" Burt Reynolds asks his bride. You nod and smile.

"We'll still need to see that ID," the cop says.

"Yours, too," the other cop says to Bobby B, who pulls out, unbelievably, an Arizona driver's license and hands it over. You pull out your freshly minted Arizona license with your lovable mug and the same last name and address as the oncologist.

"Andrews?" the cop says, looking at you.

You smile and think about the oncologist pacing hard by now.

Burt Reynolds chimes in with, "Actually we're engaged. OK, you got me: engaged to be engaged."

The cops all of a sudden seem disinterested, handing back the fake licenses. "Just keep the yelling down." And just like that, they're gone.

Minutes later, here's what Bobby B says after you find a place to pause about 50 yards away from the metal detectors where the cops just shook you down.

"Yer a right tidy package, Jet."

Your hands are sticky with sweat, your throat dry. You and Bobby B are trying to act nonchalant like the almost happily engaged couple you are, but you feel completely conspicuous and exposed. Peeing yourself is still a strong possibility. But through a smile you say, "Burt Reynolds?"

Bobby B's brogue is back with a vengeance. "It came from razor-sharp wit and always thinking four steps ahead in this game. Pick a name that will immediately break someone's focus and then be able to pull out the proper state given the situation. I could have given him California, Nevada or Oregon, too. Any western state. I knew you would be carrying 'Arizona.'"

"And what pill did I just swallow?"

Bobby B shrugs his shoulders. "Nothing harmful. You'll probably start to feel very relaxed if you haven't already."

"What was it?"

"Just a wee Valium to calm your nerves. But more importantly, you are a cheeky bird."

"Meaning what?"

"Meaning I cannae believe you drove across the Mojave Desert in a stolen nine one one and then all the way here with the heat coming down." He let out a laugh. "American women. Precious."

"Well, anyway."

You know he just saved your neck when he could have turned and walked away. He risked everything to come back for you. Bobby B just showed you his true colors.

"Thank you," you say. "Thanks for what you just did."

"Achh," he says. "Don't mention it. Does that mean you'll finally give it up? Personal erotic services in exchange for my stunning levels of chivalry?"

You laugh and then scowl and then smile again. Bobby B nods and gives you a wink.

"Let me tell you where——"

"I couldnae care less about that package, Jet. Tainted all to hell and back. I'm no going anywhere near that one."

"So it will just sit there until... what?"

"You wipe it clean like I said?"

You nod.

"So let it sit. They'll find it inside of a week and probably even get it back to its rightful owner, no damage save a few hundred extra miles."

You start to tell him about the smashed-up rearend and busted window, but realize these are now irrelevant details. The car's black-market value is now zero-point-zero.

"So everything's cool then?" you ask.

Bobby B looks at you and smiles. "Always after the dosh."

Just standing here near him and all the security makes you fidget. Come on, this isn't done until you get that stack of shrink-wrapped hundreds.

"You know it's a felony to transport more than $10,000 U.S. on your person on an international flight?"

You shake your head.

"So, truthfully," he says, "this will be a load off my mind. What's that?" He motions back toward security, but you don't see anything unusual.

"What's what?"

"Give me a wee hug," he says, opening his arms. You give him a good hug this time, but what about the money? "So how should we do this?"

"I don't like long goodbyes, so let's just say so long for now."

"No, I mean——"

"I know what you mean, luv," he says, backpedaling now.

"What are you doing? How are we going to do this?"

He's smiling, shaking his head, people passing between him and you now. "We already did it, luv. Cheeky bird."

"What? What's happening here? C'mon."

"Valium. It's all I had. You're already slowing down. Missing things."

"Valium? What about the——"

"Always after the dosh, luv, always after the dosh." Then he winks, turns and disappears into the crowd.

Then you see what he meant, looking down, a thick padded envelope at your feet. You reach down and pick it up, tear it open and see Bobby B's shrink-wrap. But something's off here.

Wow, you do feel pretty relaxed. That edge is disappearing. Things are a bit softer. But still: something off here.

You reach inside and thumb through the stack and then it hits you: Bobby B has added an enormous gratuity to your $15,000 shrink-wrapped. Even in the Valium fog of your brain you count an extra $50,000 flat on top of your $100,000/$50,000 split.

Now you want to run and find him and give him a hug. Maybe that's the Valium, too.

Three weeks and ten cars: that part of the deal in the rearview. You feel something physically release in your upper back, a deep knot that loosens. First Papa Jet and now Bobby B: The quality of men in your life has taken a decidedly positive turn.

No more joker right on your tail.

No more staring at every set of headlights and wondering.

No more sickening flash of red and blue against black morning sky. But you still have a lot of ground to cover.

Bagging number ten is a good start, Speed Yellow 911 mothballed in the parking garage.

But you know it's way too early to celebrate anything. No way you're out of the woods until you're on that plane and back in Phoenix.

And then the last hurdle to your new life: Double-Blind, Two-Box Lock-Up.

You pass through security no snags, $50,000 cash tucked in your pants at the front. You find your gate and a chair with a view of the planes.

You watch the guy with the orange flashlights guide a plane into the gate. You catch yourself smiling and thinking, this Valium is good stuff.

Then you think about Papa Jet in his red cowboy hat. When you see him there in your mind, a sadness rising up, your heart feeling like it's going to break.

You think about time.

Less than two hours later, the plane glides down and touches Arizona asphalt. Twenty minutes after that, you're stepping into the inferno of another September day in the desert. It seems especially brutal after the cool California air just two hours ago. Rolle is already stepping out of America's Ride *and walking this way in jean shorts and a black, sleeveless V-neck that clings to his muscled upper body. Revos perched on the end of his nose. New life or not, he still takes your breath away and makes your knees wobbly. He's walking with his arms open, palms turned up. You give him a hug, but feel guilty you're already thinking how to detach yourself from Las Palmas.*

"How's my baby girl?"

Rolle opens your door and smiles. Your emotions are all twisted together. Seeing the sweet side to Rolle breaks your heart and makes what you're about to do that much harder. Your head is foggy from all of it: the intense all-night run, no sleep and the Valium. You've come so far, but you're not done yet.

"Baby, c'mon. Let's go get ourselves some you-know-what." He's rubbing his hands together and has a bounce in his step. You're so glad this is one battle you don't have to fight today: He's ready to cash in the winning ticket. You think about how you trade three weeks and ten times for $100,000 (actually more now...), and finally, thank God, it's really time to go do this thing. The last dance in your march to freedom.

Double-Blind, Two-Box Lock-Up.

Chapter Thirty-Five

HERE'S WHAT ROLLE SAYS when he sees where the cash has been for three weeks: You're clowning me. You smile at your little inside joke, money stashed just half a block from Las Palmas apartments.

You're parked at the bank in *America's Ride*, engine and AC running full tilt and spitting out a pathetic stream of lukewarm air. Sweat's beading on your forehead as fast as you can wipe, and dripping down the middle of your back. Rolle doesn't seem to be sweating at all, as though he's somehow acclimated to this '70s Detroit ride forged before global warming.

Rolle drove you 30 minutes to a bank near Arizona State University to get the money key. Took you east on University right through the heart of campus and all the coeds in tiny shorts, saying, "See baby, this way while you were all blindfolded I had some nice diversions." You shake your head and smile, but your focus is elsewhere.

At the bank, you get the key no problem and, since the box is in your name, close out the account before directing Rolle to the bank in Phoenix. $135,000 on ice half a block from your apartment. You're minutes away, if all goes well, from starting your new life. Or at least from having the money to do so.

"All this time we been coming here?" He's laughing and shaking his head. "Right by our apartment? You had me all twisted around."

You nod, but you're nervous and tense. You have this sense that, close as you are, something is going to keep you from ever getting that money. It's all just been a dream.

Rolle says, "So from here you just drove me all around to get me confused?"

"Obviously it wasn't that tough."

"Oh baby, that's cold. That's real cold."

"So we ready to do this?" you ask, wishing you had the money key instead of Rolle. But that's the deal: you know where to get the cash, he holds the key until you get here. For the first time, you notice a cop parked across the lot. Is this how the end starts?

"That cop car there when we pulled in?" you ask.

Rolle leans forward and shrugs his shoulders and then settles back into the seat. "Ain't no big thing, baby. The illegalities all behind us. Now we ain't doing nothing wrong except making a little withdrawal. Speaking of which, I'd like to make a little deposit." You look over to see him smiling.

"Rolle, no." You're running on zero sleep, caffeine, adrenaline and Valium, and dripping with sweat in a 170-degree black van, and he wants to do that? Just... no.

"Why not, baby?"

You don't even bother explaining. You're out of the van. You have a white, plastic grocery sack tucked under your arm because that's what Rolle brought to pick up $135,000. You hear the driver's side door open and slam. You're five minutes away now from holding your $100,000 cash. Inside the air-conditioned lobby, Rolle signs the little card and the lady takes you into the bank vault.

"You can see now?" the bank lady asks.

"Say what?" Rolle says, forgetting.

You nudge him and say, "Yeah, isn't it great. All better." You can't remember ever meeting this lady, so she must have seen you come in with Rolle when his eyes were bandaged.

"Was it painful?" The lady's way too interested.

You look at Rolle. "Was it painful, sweetheart?"

"Not so bad, really. Heals right up."

You find the box and point it out to the lady, who asks, "Will you need a room?"

"Yes, please."

Rolle produces the key and the lady inserts it along with hers and opens the little metal door. You and Rolle both reach for the box, hands bumping, and he lets you grab the handle and pull. Your palms are sticky, your heart racing. You think about the cop you saw out in the lobby and wonder if he'd take an interest in $135,000 cash stowed in a safe-deposit box.

All you can think about is the freedom, but a different freedom than what you dreamed three weeks ago. The freedom of never putting yourself in this situation again. You follow the lady into the private room, and when she leaves, Rolle flips open the box and starts tossing the bundles onto the table.

"Rolle, don't. Might be cameras." When you say it you look into all four corners of the room, but don't see anything. Still. Don't get cocky now.

"Relax, baby. We home free all the way."

He wasn't the one out on the road ten times: That kind of talk makes you extremely nervous.

$135,000 doesn't look like much, really. Not like big piles of cash to dump on the bed and toss in the air. Each $15,000 bundle is still shrink-wrapped the way Bobby B handed them to you. Nine bundles with fifteen $100 bills in each.

"Still think I should get half," he's saying.

"Yeah, why don't you try driving just one of those cars, and we'll see what you think then."

"C'mon. Ain't no big thing, baby."

You're mostly ignoring him, stuffing your six bundles in the white plastic bag and dumping your purse on the table, then putting the cash on the bottom and piling everything back in on top. Rolle doesn't even bother with the bag, just sticks the three bundles (you already gave him $5,000 and took your $10,000 from today) in his front shorts pockets and pulls his shirt over. You start to ask him if he should conceal the cash better and then decide you're too tired. Whatever.

Back in the lobby, Rolle closes the account while you wait and try to look inconspicuous, which only makes you feel more conspicuous. Right as you look up at the cop he looks this way. He's standing with his thumbs hooked in his thick belt. You smile and give him a little wave and think, what an idiot you are. Why did you do that? You can't tell if he even noticed your wave.

Remain calm.

That rent-a-cop doesn't know anything about anything.

That rent-a-cop has no idea you're about to walk with $150,000 cash from running ten cars to California. All of it just below the Altoids and ibuprofen and hairspray.

After Rolle is finished, he stands and you start walking together. Gliding by the cop you give him a little head nod and a smile and your heart speeds up as though you'll feel the cop grabbing you from behind right before you step out of the bank and into your new life. You're certain it's all about to end, quietly, here in the bank lobby half a block from Las Palmas.

Except you don't feel anyone grab your arm as Rolle pushes open the first set of doors, into the airlock, and you follow him until you're standing in the blazing sun and thinking, that's it; you did it. Rolle is giggling, dancing as he walks to the van.

"Stop it," you say without looking back, certain the cop is taking an interest in your every move. "Be cool."

"I am cool, baby. Ain't nothing wrong with doing a little celebratory dance." Then he yells back toward the bank, "Right Mr. Policeman?"

You just shake your head and go, that answers your question. You were thinking again about maybe you don't have to walk away to start your new life. Maybe you can build on the good parts, and if you're committed he'll come around. But you know if you don't take your money and walk away today when you're feeling strong, you never will.

You watch him walk to his side of *America's Ride* and climb in, a sadness rising in your chest as you take a deep breath. Takes all your inner resolve now to remind you why you left the East and then started running cars three weeks ago. Asking yourself over and over as you climb back into the scorching van: Are you strong enough to walk away? Can you finally make a stand for you without some man clouding the picture?

Your head starts to spin from the heat, and your stomach tightens into those nasty knots. Forehead soaked. Palms sticky.

Then you feel a surge of anger and somehow snap yourself back, a hot flash of adrenaline pumping strength.

Midnight tonight, start of your new life.

Chapter Thirty-Six

DEEP WICKED FREAKY.

Says how Papa Jet falls asleep and never wakes up. The morning after number ten he seemed OK. A little tired, but not ready to go yet. He was even able to tell a couple stories as his Glen Campbell cassette played on the boombox. Gentle on My Mind. Then he got sleepy, and you promised you'd return the next morning for another visit, which you did: two hot coffees and glazed doughnuts. But Papa Jet had already quietly slipped away in the wee hours. Nick Sands would have called you at Las Palmas, but he wasn't working. Your number didn't get passed to the other staff.

Time is for you, time is against you.

Papa Jet goes 77 years.

Says how you headed west to escape your life and ended up back where you started, how you find out about Papa Jet same week he's scheduled to die, same week you decide to start boosting cars. Says how you found the missing puzzle piece to the three mystery words.

Although you only knew him for a few days, the tears keep coming, a dark sadness that seems endless. Then, hour by hour, the more you cry, you slowly climb out of the darkness until you can see that a few days with Papa Jet opened something inside you. You handle the final arrangements according to Papa Jet's wishes, a will he wrote before the stroke and gave to Nick Sands at Silvercrest:

Please, when I'm gone, just a simple cremation is all I want. Nothing fancy. I don't want anyone to cry because I lived one hell of a good life. The last thing is, and I'm putting Nick in charge of this because he's the only one around this hell-hole who knows what's what. So anyway, just scatter my ashes someplace nice outside. I don't want to be stuck in some damn container. I'll go out how I came in: free. Nick you choose where because you're as close to family as I've got. That's it.

Says how you pack up the rest of your clothes and drive to California without worrying if the headlights in the rearview are attached to a California Highway Patrol car. You laugh to yourself thinking, you are not a car thief, official or otherwise, because... You are no longer a car thief, official or otherwise. Period. The drive brings back all the insanity, but not in a way you can't handle. Almost as though you can laugh watching the old you doing crazy things as though it were years ago.

Silent flashes of red and blue in the rearview.

A car door slamming back there.

Footsteps and a flashlight beam coming this way.

You breathe easy and relax. From the confines of a legally rented black Ford Taurus, none of that can touch you anymore. You laugh when you think about goatee Kim and Barney Fife and ponder a stop in Indio for a cup of coffee. And then you decide against it: Your new life is waiting.

Says how for the first time in your life, you really are free. Leaving Rolle wasn't as hard as you'd built it up to be in your mind. Just went in, packed up your clothes and left while he was out with his crew. No big drama, no final showdown, just a short note thanking him for everything. You had to fight off some guilt for not telling Rolle about the extra $50,000 or sharing it with him. After all, you would still be back at $0 if not for Rolle. But then you realized that was stupid because it was you who took all the risk. And there's no doubt that Bobby B wanted every penny of that extra money going into your purse, not to Rolle.

So with that resolved in your mind, just like that you and Rolle were done. You still feel a weird mixture of sadness, knowing you'll miss him, and yet, relief. Rolle is a good guy—just not *your* guy. He's not your new life.

Says how you'll get a job as a waitress for starters and see what's next and no matter what, you'll never go back. Not to anything that steals a part of you that you never get back. Not ever. That's a promise you made to Papa Jet the time you spilled your guts. You'll do it for him; you'll do it for you.

Says how when you get to LA you drive straight to Santa Monica and Palisades Park overlooking the ocean. Same route you ran in number ten, Turbo 911. How Nick Sands said he knows Papa Jet would want you to choose, and this is the first place that pops into your head. The high cliff overlooking the shimmering Pacific Ocean, a place of peace and a launching-off point for both you and Papa Jet. How you unscrew the lid and gently shake out the remains and watch them flutter down toward the ocean. You find yourself smiling when you think about your straight-up grandfather.

Then you just sit and stare at the ocean for awhile, wiping your eyes and laughing about how much Papa Jet loved his country music and playing the horses, how his last night at the track he even picked a few winners. How you made sure he didn't die alone at Silvercrest.

Says how now you have a reason *not* to do escort or run stolen cars across black desert, something simple to hold onto that's not much, but at least it's all yours. You figure you can stretch your cash for five years, with careful budgeting and planning and a part-time job, which is enough to get through school and launch whatever career you decide to pursue.

Says how you sense you're finally free to enjoy the good, and strong enough to handle the bad, and mostly how names read from a horse-racing program by Papa Jet changes everything. During a short lucid moment the morning after number ten, he told you about his granddaughter Jenna. Back east, in the small white house, you used to sit on his lap as he read each name from the horse-racing program, which drove your mom nuts—*That's not appropriate for a child!*—but made for good laughs and a special bond. Papa Jet goes 77 years and could rattle off names in Silvercrest like his hair was still black as midnight.

Mountain Man It's Like I Said

Potato Farmer in the Sky

AR's Fly Fisherman Wonder

deep wicked freaky

One-in-three odds wiped away by certainty. The freedom and awareness of knowing who you are and being OK with who stares back when you look into a mirror.

A cartoon nickname from your grandfather.

The start of your new life.

LANDON J. NAPOLEON is the award-winning and critically acclaimed author of fiction and nonfiction books. He earned a bachelor's degree in journalism from Arizona State University, a master's degree from University of Glasgow in Scotland, and has been an author for more than two decades.

His debut novel *ZigZag* received starred reviews, was a Barnes & Noble "Discover Great New Writers" finalist (1999), and was translated into multiple foreign editions and adapted for a motion picture (Franchise Pictures, 2002) starring John Leguizamo, Oliver Platt, and Wesley Snipes.

His nonfiction biography *Burning Shield: The Jason Schechterle Story* was a 2014 "Arizona Republic Recommends" selection. Interweaving narratives of human triumph, medical marvels, police procedure, and high-stakes legal showdowns, this "inspiring true story" (Kirkus Reviews) chronicles the triumph of a rare human being with an undeniable will to live.

www.landonjnapoleon.com